Barney and the

UFO

Books by Margaret Goff Clark

Barney and the UFO

Mystery in the Flooded Museum

Mystery of Sebastian Island

Death at Their Heels

Mystery Horse

Mystery at Star Lake

Adirondack Mountain Mystery

Mystery of the Missing Stamps

Danger at Niagara

Freedom Crossing

The Mystery of Seneca Hill

The Mystery of the Buried Indian Mask

Mystery of the Marble Zoo

Benjamin Banneker

John Muir

Their Eyes on the Stars

BARNEY AND THE UFO

Margaret Goff Clark

Illustrated by Ted Lewin

DODD, MEAD & COMPANY· NEW YORK

ACKNOWLEDGMENTS

The author wishes to thank: WILLIAM BARAN, Chairman, Science Department, Niagara Wheatfield Central School, for checking the manuscript; GLENN LEATHERSICH, member of the Early American Industries Association, for his information on old barns.

1   2   3   4   5   6   7   8   9   10

Library of Congress Cataloging in Publication Data

Clark, Margaret Goff.
    Barney and the UFO.

    SUMMARY: Barney is afraid to tell his foster parents
that he has seen a UFO behind the house even when a hasty
promise to a space boy leads him into trouble.
    [1. Unidentified flying objects—Fiction.   2. Science
fiction.   3. Foster home care—Fiction]   I. Lewin,
Ted.   II. Title.
PZ7.C5487Bar   [Fic]   79-52046
ISBN 0-396-07711-0

To my creative editor, Rosemary Casey,
who saw the mist and who knew that
Tibbo had to be a space boy

CONTENTS

1	Unseen Eyes	9
2	Dick Williams	14
3	A Home Worth Keeping	19
4	The UFO	27
5	Barney Searches for Evidence	36
6	A Visitor from Outer Space	41
7	The Lonely Secret	50
8	Barney Is a Hero	55
9	Trouble	63
10	Tibbo Comes Again	73
11	The Skeleton Barn	84
12	How Far to Ornam?	91
13	A Strange Magnetic Power	102
14	Son!	109
15	Runaway Truck	117
16	Invisible Space Ship	121
17	Tibbo Is Stubborn	128
18	A Strange Story	138
19	The Space Ship Returns	145
20	Farewell	152

1 ▬▬▬ UNSEEN EYES

It was time to leave for the school bus.

Barney Galloway stood in the front hall with his lunch pail in one hand and his math book in the other, trying to gather up the courage to open the door. After the strangeness of yesterday, he couldn't bear to go out. And yet he didn't want to miss school, not on the last day before summer vacation. He knew he had passed, but he still had to get his report card.

His four-year-old brother Scott was crawling around in the living room, pushing a toy dump truck. The little tow-headed boy, a small copy of Barney, wheeled over and wrapped his arms around one of his brother's legs.

"Stay home, Barney," he pleaded. "I'll let you play with my space ship."

The space ship looked something like a Frisbee with a bowl upside down on top of it. When you pushed a button, the ship lighted up. Then a small door opened and two plastic men in space suits slid out on a tiny runway.

It was Scott's favorite toy. Mr. Crandall had brought it home for him a couple of weeks ago.

Barney crouched so he was on Scott's level. "Thanks, Tiger. I sure wish I didn't have to leave." He looked at the clock that stood on top of the bookcase. "Yipes! I'll miss the bus!"

He thrust his lunch pail under his arm and pulled open the door. Then, taking a deep breath, he ran out and slammed the door behind him.

For a moment he thought everything was going to be all right today. The air felt soft and good, just the way it always had been—until yesterday.

As he hurried down the front walk, his eight-month-old Irish terrier, Finn McCool—Finn for short—ran after him, leaping on stiff legs and giving little barks of joy. The dog never followed him when he left for school. Why was he coming with him today? Sometimes it seemed as if Finn could read his mind. Perhaps the dog knew he needed a friend.

"Come on, then," urged Barney. "Stay with me, boy."

Finn was another of Mr. Crandall's gifts. He had given the young dog to Barney the day the two orphaned brothers had come to live with him and his wife. That was a month and a half ago.

"You're our son now," the man had said as he put Finn into Barney's arms. "We hope you'll be happy

10

here because we want to adopt you and Scott.''

But there was a wait of six months before the adoption could become final, and Barney was afraid to hope. He had been disappointed before.

The Galloway boys' new home was a mile south of Pineville, a valley town in the foothills of the Catskill Mountains of New York State.

Barney had to go a quarter of a mile to the school bus stop, along a narrow road which for the most part led through open country. Sometimes he walked with Kara MacDougall, a girl a year younger than he, who lived almost half a mile beyond the Crandalls' house. Today he didn't see her.

He started out at a trot with Finn close behind him They rounded a bend in the road and crossed a wooden-floored bridge over a stream. Still everything was all right.

They had passed through a small, sweet-scented pine woods when suddenly Barney knew that things were not okay. His heart began to pound and his hands were sweaty.

The air around him felt—funny. As if it had electricity in it. His skin tingled the way it did when his hands and feet went to sleep. The top of his head began to prickle even through his thick blond hair, and he was sure someone was watching him.

This was the way it was yesterday, too, whenever he

was outdoors. The prickling didn't really hurt, but it was such a strange sensation, it bothered him. It was weird, that's what it was.

Now, searching for the person who was spying on him, he glanced to the right at a gray-shingled house with the shades still drawn. The lady who lived there liked to sleep late. Not a curtain moved in the front windows.

Across the road was only a vacant lot.

No one was walking ahead of him and there was no car in sight. When he looked over his shoulder he could see only Finn, prancing at his heels with his short, sassy tail in the air.

As he hurried on, Barney told himself no one could be looking at him. The grass in the fields was early-summer short. No one could be hiding there. But he still had the sensation that eyes were noting his every step. Only now he began to think the watcher was overhead, staring down at him.

Barney looked up. The sky was a clear, robin's-egg blue without any clouds. Not a plane or a jet stream marked its emptiness.

What's the matter with me? he worried. No one *could* be watching him. It was all his imagination, and that was really scary.

Finn McCool stood up and put his front paws on Barney's leg as if asking what was the matter. He stayed there with his bright, beady eyes on his master's face while Barney gave him an absent-minded pat. Then Barney pulled his lunch pail out from under his arm and took hold of the handle.

As soon as he touched the handle, a sharp prickle in the palm of his hand almost made him let go of the pail. The metal handle seemed to be full of needles.

At the same moment Finn dropped to the ground and started to yip the way he had done last week when a bee stung him. He fled back toward home with his tail down, whimpering all the way.

It wasn't like Finn to be afraid. Young as he was, he'd stand up to any creature that challenged him.

Barney didn't have time to follow him. The dog would be all right. He'd soon be home, and Mrs. Crandall would let him in. This time it certainly was not a bee that had stung him.

Though the top of his head and his hand still tingled, Barney was comforted. Whatever was bugging him, it wasn't his imagination. Finn had felt it, too.

2 🗲🗲🗲 DICK WILLIAMS

The bus was coming. Barney burst into a run, his lunch pail under his arm rattling as he thudded up the street. He hated to think of walking the two miles to school with the air stinging his skin like this.

The bus came to a halt, and Kara, the only one at the bus stop, climbed aboard. The door closed behind her. Barney waved frantically, hoping someone would see him puffing up the road.

To his relief, the bus did not move away. The horn gave two beeps that meant "Hurry up!"

The door wheezed open, and Barney staggered up the steps. As soon as he was inside, the strange feeling in the air was gone.

The bus was three-quarters full, but Barney found an empty seat near the front.

As he slid over next to the window he saw a familiar tall, long-legged figure coming into view.

The driver had already closed the door and was shifting gears.

"Wait!" cried Barney. "Dick Williams is almost here!"

The driver sighed and opened the door again.

Dick could really run when he had to, thought Barney. It wasn't often that he moved quickly. Right now the forward thrust of his head, the backward flight of his brown hair, and his fast-moving thin legs made him look like a heron about to take to the air.

Barney liked Dick, but he was a little in awe of him. Everyone knew that he was a brain. He got A's without even trying. The teachers were always after him to study.

"There's no limit to what you could do, Dick Williams," the English teacher, Mrs. Redding, had said. "I believe you could be a scientist or a mathematician or an inventor, or whatever you want to be, if you'd just do a little more work. Why can't you be like Barney?" she demanded. "He always has his homework in on time and he does more book reports than you do."

Barney ducked his head and tried to be invisible. There was nothing to make a guy unpopular like having the teacher point you out as a good example.

Besides, Mrs. Redding wasn't being fair to Dick. He did plenty of studying about things he was interested in, like space travel, for instance. In science class he had given a report on "Visitors from Other Worlds" that had even surprised the teacher, Mr. Wexel.

Dick leaped up the steps and said "Thanks" to the bus driver. A moment later he sat down beside Barney with his lunch pail on his lap.

Barney couldn't believe his luck. Usually Dick sat in the rear of the bus with some of his pals. This was a great chance to get better acquainted with him. But what could he say to a real brain? He certainly couldn't tell him about the strange prickly feeling in the air.

Dick didn't wait for Barney to start the conversation.

"Hey, Barney," he said. "I hear you like to play ball. Softball, I mean."

"How'd you hear that?"

Dick grinned, showing square white teeth. " 'My Favorite Sport' by Barney Galloway. Mrs. Redding put your comp on the bulletin board."

"Yeah," Barney admitted. "I forgot about that. I played quite a lot in Buffalo where I used to live. We kids had a team." He didn't explain that then he had been living in an orphanage because his parents had been killed in an auto accident. In those days he had read, practiced, and played softball every possible moment because it helped him blot out his terrible loneliness.

"How'd you like to play Saturday afternoon?" asked Dick.

Barney was surprised, but he didn't hesitate. "Sure." That would be day after tomorrow. He'd get out his old

16

softball and bat, and try hitting some flies.

"Some of us started a team about a month ago—the Pineville Patriots. We practice about three times a week and we're not too bad." Dick didn't look as if he were bragging, but as if he were just stating a fact. "We have our first game Saturday with the Valmora Vultures."

Barney's hopes soared. He had heard about the Patriots. If he did okay Saturday, probably he'd be asked to join the team. He had really missed playing since he had moved here.

Dick went on. "You'll be filling in for me. I play right field. I'm going to Albany today with Dad and Mom to visit my aunt and we won't be back until Saturday night."

"Oh, all right." Now Barney knew why Dick had sat down with him. He needed a substitute. And what about his chances for being asked to join the team? wondered Barney. If he was just filling in for Dick, they might not need another player. Well, anyway, it would be fun to play, even in one game. "Where do I go?" he asked.

"The game starts at one-thirty in that field behind the firehall. Better get there ahead of time. And tell Jake I sent you. He's the captain and he's in charge because so far we don't have a coach. We've been looking for one, but we can't find anybody who has time to work with us."

"I'll be there," agreed Barney.

17

As they continued to talk, Barney began to feel at ease with Dick. He even dared to hope that they might become friends.

As yet he didn't have a close friend nearby. Not like Howie, his pal who lived next door to the orphanage back in Buffalo. He could have told Howie about the funny feeling in the air. Howie wouldn't laugh or think he was making it up.

The bus swung into the half-moon of driveway in front of the school. It came to a jolting halt near the main entrance.

Since Barney and Dick were near the front of the bus, they were among the first to get out. Dick was ahead of Barney, and when he came to the exit, he leaped out, shouting, "See you later!"

Just as his feet landed on the ground, he dropped his lunch pail. He snatched it up and tucked it under his arm. Then he charged for the school like a scared rabbit.

Barney gazed after him with growing excitement. It was unusual enough to see Dick run when he didn't have to. But besides that, was there some reason why Dick had dropped his lunch pail and then tucked it under his arm?

The pail, like Barney's, was plastic with a metal handle. Was it possible that Dick, too, had felt the electric prickle of the air?

3 ☗☗☗ A HOME WORTH KEEPING

Barney rushed into school after Dick, hoping he would have a chance to talk with him alone before the bell rang.

Once inside the door, he expected to see the tall, lean boy with the straight brown hair ahead of him on the way to their classroom.

Instead, he caught a glimpse of him in the corridor to his left. A moment later he disappeared into the main office.

The final bell had rung when Dick came in and gave a note to the teacher before he sat down.

All morning Barney waited without success for an opportunity to talk to Dick. Finally at lunchtime he found him seated at an otherwise empty table in the cafeteria.

Barney pulled out a chair next to him. "Okay if I sit here?"

"Sure." Dick slid a sandwich out of its plastic bag. "Corned beef on rye," he commented. "That's not bad."

Barney was hungry, but for once something was more important than food.

He blurted out, "Does the air ever feel funny to you?"

Dick swallowed a bite of sandwich and looked at Barney with surprise written all over his narrow face. "No," he gulped. "How do you mean, funny?"

"Well," Barney said hesitantly, "prickly—like needles—" He stopped abruptly.

A tall, well-built boy with black curly hair was approaching their table, carrying a small carton of milk and a bag lunch. Barney knew him only by sight.

The newcomer pulled out a chair across from the two boys. In a strong, hearty voice he exclaimed, "Hey, Dick! I hear you're missing the game tomorrow. What's the big idea?"

"Cool it," said Dick. "I have a substitute for you. Jake, this is Barney Galloway. He's played a lot of softball in Buffalo where he came from and he says he'll fill in for me."

Jake nodded a greeting and looked Barney over. "Ever play right field?"

"Yeah. Sometimes. But mostly I played catcher."

Jake seemed pleased. "Guess you'll do. Why can't you come, Dick?"

Barney waited, on edge, while Jake stayed, eating his lunch and talking about the team, mostly to Dick. It was

20

hard to imagine Dick playing ball. He usually was so slow moving, but he *had* run fast twice today. Barney was glad his new friend said nothing to Jake about prickly air. He was sorry he had mentioned it in the first place.

At twelve-thirty Dick closed his lunch pail and stood up. "Have to go now. Mom's picking me up."

Jake jumped to his feet. "I'll walk you to the door."

"Okay." Dick looked back at Barney. "See you later. Good luck tomorrow."

Barney felt heavy with disappointment. Obviously Dick hadn't noticed anything unusual about the air. It was just by chance that he had dropped his lunch pail and then put it under his arm.

Barney's face became warm as he thought about his conversation with Dick. "Does the air ever feel funny?" What a dumb question to ask someone he scarcely knew.

When Mrs. Redding passed out the report cards, Barney felt more cheerful. His marks were much better than he had dared hope. He looked forward to showing the card to the Crandalls.

Walking down the road from the bus stop with Kara that afternoon, Barney felt more carefree. His skin wasn't prickly. School was over until September, and tomorrow he was going to play ball.

As if reading his mind, Kara said, "I hear you're

playing at the firehall field tomorrow.''

"Yeah. How'd you know?''

She gave him a quick glance from honest, dark eyes. "Everyone knows.''

Barney grinned. "I wonder who my press agent is.''

"I guess I'll go to the game. Are you a good player?''

"I dunno. Haven't played since last fall.'' He wished he could practice with the team. He'd hate to make a fool of himself in front of Kara. Well, he'd do the best he could.

Mrs. Crandall had the radio on and was doing dance steps in the kitchen as she moved from sink to stove to work counter. She and her husband were always dancing, it seemed to Barney. They knew all the latest steps and sometimes after dinner they'd practice.

Both of them were crazy about music. Mrs. Crandall could play any piece on the piano and her husband was great on the trumpet, though his job was working as a lineman for the telephone company.

Barney waited until Mrs. Crandall paused at the sink and then he said, "Hi,'' and held out his report card.

She whirled around, her straight black hair flying out from her face. "Hi, Barney! I didn't hear you come in.''

She wiped her hands and took the card.

Barney leaned against the kitchen counter and waited.

22

Mrs. Crandall was pretty, he thought. Her face had an alive look as if she was always expecting something nice to happen. He knew she'd be pleased with the card, but she surprised him when she ran over and kissed him on one cheek and then the other.

"That's what the French do when they award the Legion of Honor," she said.

Barney's cheeks were red, but he couldn't help smiling.

"Wonderful marks!" she declared, and then added ruefully, "I never got a card like that when I was in school."

For once Barney forgot to be formal and polite. "No kidding!" he exclaimed.

Mrs. Crandall looked delighted. "No kidding!" she repeated. "I was just an average student."

Embarrassed, Barney said, "I'm sorry. I didn't mean—"

"Don't apologize. I love it when you forget to be stiff and proper. Alex and I aren't like that, you know."

That was true, thought Barney as he went up to his room. Mrs. Crandall and her husband were always joking with each other or laughing at nothing, it seemed to him. He had never known people like that and he didn't know how to enter into their fun.

His own parents had been serious. But they didn't have it easy, he defended them in his mind. They had come to the United States from Ireland before he was born, and they both had worked hard. Often they had told him that they had come because there was more opportunity to get ahead in this country. They had said it would be a better place for him and Scott to grow up. That was one reason why Barney had wanted to stay in the United States, even after an aunt in Ireland offered to take him and his brother. Besides, she had a big family of her own and she didn't need two more mouths to feed.

Still deep in thought, Barney sat down on the edge of his bed and stared out the window. It faced south, giving him a view of the two-car garage to his left, the back yard, and beyond that a meadow that sloped gently up toward Mount Casper, which was really more of a hill than a mountain. Far to the right was the Crandalls' old, unused barn.

Only inches below his windowsill was the almost level roof of the back porch. Sometime, just for kicks, he was going to crawl onto that roof and see if he could make it to the ground.

Barney glanced contentedly around his room. Mrs. Crandall had sure done a lot of work to fix it the way he'd like it.

She had been so nice about his report card and everything, Barney was tempted to go back downstairs and tell her about the prickle of his skin and the feeling of

24

being watched. But she might think he had something wrong with him, some rare disease, for instance. No, he couldn't talk to the Crandalls about his problem. He didn't want to do anything to worry them.

Nothing must happen this time to keep him and Scott from being adopted. Barney knew from experience how hard it was to find a home.

After the death of their parents, he and Scott had been in the orphanage for two years. It had seemed that almost everyone who came there looking for someone to adopt took a baby or a young child. Three times someone had wanted Scott, and once a farmer and his wife had picked out Barney.

But each time Barney had held out for a place for both him and his brother.

One couple had agreed to take both of them on trial, but after a month they had brought them back. "We like you and Scott," the woman had told Barney, "but we want just one *little* boy."

Barney had almost lost hope, but then the Crandalls had come all the way from the southeastern part of New York State. They had said they would take the two brothers.

Even this time something had happened to make Barney fearful.

He was in his dormitory packing his few belongings when one of the older boys had sat down on his bed.

"You'll be back again." The boy spoke with assurance.

Barney had looked at him sharply, afraid. "Not this time!"

"Oh, yes, you will," insisted the other boy. "I heard them talking in the office."

"What'd they say?"

"You'll find out." The boy had walked away, leaving Barney shaking with helpless anger.

Well, they were still here. Scott was putting on weight and he was calling Mrs. Crandall "Mom."

Barney wasn't going to let those strange prickles or anything else blow the chance he and his brother had to be part of a family again.

4 彡彡彡 THE UFO

That night Barney awakened suddenly from a sound sleep. His eyes flew open to the cool darkness of the room.

What had awakened him? He felt frightened, and he didn't know why. All he could remember was a sound like a powerful wind. But the curtains at the open window beside his bed were not even moving.

He couldn't hear anything now, not even a car going by, but that was not unusual. This house, alone on a country road, was always quiet at night. After a month and a half here, Barney's ears no longer listened for the city sounds of traffic, the wail of fire and police sirens.

Barney rubbed his face and then his bare arms. There was that prickly feeling again. This was the first time he had felt it when he was indoors.

Since he had come here to live he had felt safe any time, day or night. But right now he was uneasy. Something strange was going on.

He tried to tell himself everything was all right. The prickling would go away. And if anything unusual was happening outside, Finn would be barking.

Go to sleep! his mind told him.

Stay awake and find out what's up, insisted his heart, hammering at his ribs.

Quietly Barney slid out of bed and dropped to his knees beside the window.

To his amazement the back yard and meadow had vanished under a cloud of mist that was unlike anything he had ever seen before. It moved as if it were alive, and it sparkled like star shine. To his left the tip of the garage roof thrust up like an island. Far off to his right the lonely old barn looked like an ark afloat in a white sea.

As Barney gazed down from his window, the shimmering mist seemed to pull him. He had to get closer to it and find out what made it shine. There was no moon, and although the sky was full of stars, they weren't bright enough to make the meadow glimmer like snow on a sunny day.

He *had* to go outside! The mist was drawing him like a magnet. He could creep down the stairs and hope he wouldn't awaken the Crandalls or Scott or Finn. Or he could go out the window as he'd been wanting to do, anyway.

The Crandalls' room was on the far corner of the

house from his, so they shouldn't hear him. Scott was a sound sleeper. Finn might hear him, whatever he did. He'd have to take that chance.

The screen in his window was the kind that could be raised. Cautiously he slid it upward and climbed out.

When he stood up straight with his bare feet clinging easily to the shingles of the roof, he felt like King Kong on top of the Empire State Building.

The mist covered all of the low-lying land as far as he could see. Trees thrust their branches above it, and Mount Casper loomed like a dark giant emerging from a foamy sea.

Barney walked cautiously to the front right-hand corner of the roof where he had noticed a sturdy drain-pipe that he might be able to climb down. Just as he started to kneel to examine the pipe, he caught a glimpse of something near the old barn, the distance of half a city block away. Something that moved.

At first it seemed to be part of the mist, but then it lifted upward, so it was in front of the black woods.

Barney drew in a sharp breath.

The thing was a huge, silver-colored ball with a ring around the middle. No wonder he had not seen it before. It matched the color of the mist. Now it hung in the air looking like an ornament for a giant's Christmas tree. No lights shone from it, but its silver color made it stand out against the dark background.

While he watched, the ball floated to the left, coming nearer to him.

Until now Barney had not been afraid. But as the ball drew closer, he realized how plainly he could be seen by anyone who might be inside the strange object.

He backed up the roof toward the open window, but his curiosity was stronger than his fear.

When the thing was lined up behind the house, the silver ball began to travel forward, gliding smoothly above the mist. It came directly toward Barney.

What was it going to do? Was it going to ram the house? Or perhaps it would zap him with a ray gun. Frightened as he was, Barney could not move. The silver object was so close he could see that the ball was rotating with a faint whirring noise while the ring around it remained steady.

For thirty seconds the sphere hovered at the edge of the meadow while Barney remained frozen, scarcely breathing. Though he could see no opening in the craft, he had an unpleasant feeling that someone was looking out at him. The prickles were stronger than he had ever felt them.

Suddenly the ball shot upward. It rose so fast he couldn't follow it with his eyes. But as it left, he heard a rush of air, like a gust of wind. Like the sound that had awakened him.

A moment later the wind of its going reached Barney.

It blew his pajamas against his body and tossed his hair wildly.

Then the wind stopped as if it had been turned off. When Barney glanced at the meadow, he could see that the shining mist had disappeared as quickly as the silver ball, leaving him in darkness on the roof.

Barney drew a long, shaky breath.

That was a UFO! It had to be. It didn't look exactly like the ones he had seen on TV, but that didn't matter. People saw all kinds. This one was small, not more than fifteen or twenty feet across, including the ring.

He steadied himself against the wall of the house while he tilted his head so he could look farther into the sky. For several minutes he searched the heavens, but the UFO had vanished without leaving a trace.

Barney felt as if he might explode with excitement. He had to tell someone about the thing he had seen. Eager to share his experience with the Crandalls, he crawled back through his window and lowered the screen.

The dark house folded its arms around him. It was completely silent. There was not even a whimper from Finn in the kitchen. How strange that he had not been aware of the silver craft in the back yard.

Barney started across the room and then came to a halt before he had gone more than two or three steps.

How could he wake the Crandalls in the middle of the

night to tell them he had seen a UFO? If they were his own father and mother, it would be different. But so far they weren't even his adopted parents.

The UFO would be as hard for them to believe as the prickles and his feeling of being watched. In his desire to talk about the silver ball, he even considered telling Scott. Although he was only four, Scott would understand about UFO's, but he'd be sure to make so much noise he'd wake up their foster parents.

All at once Barney realized that his skin no longer prickled. Did the UFO have something to do with that? Had it sent some kind of electricity toward him?

But other times when he had felt that mysterious tingling, he hadn't seen any UFO.

Finally he dropped onto his bed, even though he knew he could not sleep.

His thoughts went around and around as he relived his strange experience. What had caused the mist? Where had that UFO come from? Why had it come here? Was someone inside really looking out at him?

The way the silver ball had moved, it seemed to be maneuvering so it could get a good look at him.

How beautiful that ball was! It had a magical look.

Thinking soberly, he wondered if he should tell anyone what he had seen. In the TV shows, reporting a UFO led to all kinds of problems. If word got out that he had seen one, some people would say he had made it up. Reporters would phone and TV crews would photo-graph the hillside where he had seen the silver ball.

The Crandalls mightn't like all of that publicity.

Barney tossed around on the bed, struggling to think straight. The kids at school would be interested, but if he told them, soon the whole town, perhaps the whole world, would know.

If he told the Crandalls, would they believe him? Wouldn't they wonder why he hadn't called them in time for them to see it, too? But it had happened so fast, he had thought only of watching it.

At last he made up his mind. Like the prickles, the UFO was going to be his own secret, at least for now.

5 ㅂㅂㅂ BARNEY SEARCHES
FOR EVIDENCE

When he awakened the next morning, Barney was dismayed to discover it was eight o'clock. He'd miss the school bus for sure.

Then he remembered. Even though today was Friday, there was no school. It was over until next fall.

Getting dressed took him a long time. He kept thinking about the UFO and forgetting what he was doing. Finn McCool came up to look for him and slowed him down still more by grabbing his socks and running off with them.

Before he went down to breakfast, Barney listened to the news on the local radio station, sure that someone else must have seen the silver ball. He was disappointed when there was no mention of it.

He began to wonder. Could he have imagined it? Or had the silver ball been a trick of the starlight? His memory of it was so real, he didn't see how it could have been imagination or a dream.

All during breakfast he kept wanting to tell Mrs.

Crandall what he had seen the night before. He had to remind himself, *Keep still.* She'd think he was an odd-ball.

Seeing a UFO and not being able to talk about it was torture. There was just one person to whom he could talk, one person who might believe him. Dick Williams. But he wouldn't be home until Saturday night.

In his report for science class, Dick had said that people from space were bound to try to contact Earth some day, that there were probably many planets with some kind of creatures on them who knew even more about space travel than earth people knew.

Anybody who thought like that would be ready to understand about the silver ball. And from what Barney knew of Dick, he was sure he could keep a secret.

Scott had already eaten and was watching cartoons on TV when Barney went into the living room. By promising to play ball with him later, Barney got him to give up the cartoons long enough so he could watch the news.

Mrs. Crandall said, ''I didn't know you were so interested in the news, Barney. I'm glad to see you watching it.''

As far as Barney was concerned, the news report was a failure. It did not mention a UFO.

Well, *he* had seen one!

He flipped the switch to the cartoons and Scott again

settled down happily. Now was a good time to go out and look for evidence.

Barney ran down the back steps and into the yard with Finn leaping beside him. He had the morning to himself. Mrs. Crandall would not think it strange for him to wander around the field and mountainside with his dog.

His first stop was at the edge of the meadow, where it joined the back yard. Here he studied the ground to see if the grass was blackened. As he expected, there was no sign of burned grass. He had not seen any red glare under the UFO. There had been no roar as it took off, only the rush of wind. Apparently it did not use the kind of fuel that propelled the spacecraft that had blasted off from Cape Kennedy for the moon.

Even though he retraced the route of the silver ball across the hillside, past the stone wall, and over to the old barn, he could find no real evidence. Near the barn, he thought the grass was a little flat. Finn sniffed around, but he didn't act excited.

Barney wondered if experts could discover radiation or other proof that the UFO had been there.

As long as he was nearby, he decided to take another look at the barn. He liked the old building, with its boards silvery with age.

Years ago the house and land around it had been part of a farm owned by Mr. Crandall's grandfather. But

38

now all that was left was the big house where the Crandalls lived, the stone wall, and this barn that stood alone in the meadow as if dreaming of cows and horses and a loft full of hay.

Barney wondered why the barn was so far from the house. Perhaps once there had been another house nearer the barn.

Barney slid open the wide door, letting sunlight fall across the dusty floor boards, littered with wisps of straw.

A barn owl with a face like a monkey flew silently out of the open door, so low that Barney ducked. Finn ran outside, chasing it.

Mrs. Crandall was always worrying about this barn. She said it was ready to fall apart and that some kids might get hurt climbing around in it.

Her husband kept promising to have it torn down.

"When it comes down I'd like some of that lovely old wood," Mrs. Crandall had said. "We need a family room and that will be perfect for the walls."

Mr. Crandall laughed at that. "Now I know why you want it leveled. Well, this summer Barney and I will tackle it."

The old barn didn't look too bad, Barney thought as he scuffed past the horse stalls. But it would be fun to help tear it down. Maybe he could have some of the wood to build a shack or a tree house. He had always wanted to put up a place of his own.

That night at dinner he said hesitantly, "Uh, Dick Williams—he's in my class at school—asked me to fill in for him in a ball game tomorrow."

Mr. Crandall said, "That's great, Barney. I didn't know you were a ballplayer. You ought to tell us about these things. You'll need a glove, won't you?"

"Dick left his at the firehall. I can use that."

"You need a cap, maybe?"

"No. I have one that's okay. Thank you."

"I know one thing you need." Mr. Crandall had his joking look. "An audience. Fans. Lois and Scott and I will go and root for you."

Oh, no! thought Barney. Now he'd be sure to goof it all up. He said weakly, "Thanks, but you don't have to go."

"Nothing could keep me away," said Mr. Crandall. "That's one reason I wanted a boy. So I'd have someone to cheer for at ball games."

Barney looked at him uncertainly. Was that a joke?

After dinner he read the newspaper with more care than ever before in his life. But once more he was disappointed. He did not find even a short item about a UFO.

That night he gazed out the window for a long time, hoping the UFO would return. If he saw it again he'd call the Crandalls so they could see it, too. Then nobody could say he had imagined it.

6   ☡☡☡   A VISITOR FROM OUTER SPACE

Barney fell asleep as soon as he went to bed.

In the middle of the night he dreamed that he was lost in a snowstorm. With Finn at his side he climbed over great snowdrifts. He seemed to have no coat, and his skin was stung by the icy cold.

In the distance someone was calling, "Barney! Barney! Wake up! I've come to visit you."

As he fought his way toward consciousness, Barney realized that the room was light. Brightness shone through his closed eyelids, though it couldn't be morning yet.

"Barney, wake up and talk to me."

Still drowsy, Barney thought how strange it was that he was awake and he could still hear the voice that had called in his dream. It wasn't anyone he had ever heard before. In fact, it sounded like a radio.

He opened his eyes to narrow slits. The room was full of a rosy glow, but through the window on his left he could see the dark sky, littered with stars like tossed confetti.

Barney glanced around the room. Not a single lamp was on. What made it so light?

He rubbed his face. That prickly air again. It was worse than ever before.

Suddenly he was wide awake. Last night his skin had felt like this when the UFO had come. With one leap he was out of bed and at the window. Tonight there was no shining mist, and no UFO drifted above the dark meadow.

"I thought you'd never wake up." The voice seemed to come from behind him.

The voice was in the room! Barney did not move from where he stood, facing the window. His heart was pounding so hard he could feel it in his throat. What stranger was talking to him in the middle of the night? And why hadn't Finn barked? With his sharp ears he should be able to hear the voice, even though he was in his bed in the kitchen.

Silence.

No one stirred or spoke. Barney wanted to scream, but he couldn't even squeak. He wanted to run, but his feet seemed glued to the floor. If only Finn were here, he'd feel better.

The silence went on until he could endure it no longer.

Slowly he turned around to face the bed. The voice had come from his reading corner on the far side of the room.

There was his comfortable red chair in front of the bookshelves, but no one was sitting in it.

"Where are you?" he demanded hoarsely.

"Over here." The voice spoke from the desk on the west wall to his left.

Barney turned quickly, but the desk chair was empty.

At that he became angry. He was scared half to death and someone had the nerve to tease him.

"Stop playing games!" he said indignantly.

"All right, you win. Here I am." The voice had laughter in it, and this time it was close beside him, as if the speaker were on the bed.

Barney turned again. But when he saw no one sitting on the rumpled sheets, he darted around the foot of the bed and ran for the door.

"Wait!" called the voice. "What good will it do to tell the Crandalls? They won't believe you."

Barney paused, still clutching the doorknob. "How'd you know what I was going to do?"

"You ran to the door. Of course you were going to the Crandalls' room. Now listen, I won't hurt you. I can answer a lot of your questions. Like what makes the air tingle. And what was that silver ball you saw last night."

The answer to his questions! In spite of his alarm, Barney couldn't resist that.

"Who are you?" he asked.

"I'm a boy about the same age as you, the way you measure time. My name's Tibbo."

"Tibbo! That's a funny name."

"Not any funnier than Barney." Again the voice came from the red chair in the corner. "Go back to bed. Open the door and leave it open, if you want to."

Barney pulled the door wide open. He did feel safer that way. "Mr. and Mrs. Crandall will pop in any minute," he said. He hoped they would.

"They're not likely to come," said Tibbo. "I've soundproofed their room so they won't hear us, even with your door open. I took care of your little brother's room and the kitchen, too, so your dog wouldn't start barking."

So that was why Finn hadn't made a fuss.

"You didn't do anything to hurt any of them, did you?" asked Barney anxiously.

"Of course not."

Barney returned to the bed where he sat bolt upright with his legs hanging over the edge, ready to run if necessary.

"All right, Tibbo, why can't I see you?" Barney was proud that his voice now sounded steady. "Where are you?"

44

"In a way, I'm in this room, in the red chair. All of me is here except my body."

"Ha!" said Barney. "How can you be here without your body?"

"It's something like television in reverse. I can see you, but you can't see me. Wait." The sound of the voice was again close to Barney. "I'm beside you now. Reach out your hand toward my voice. The prickles are stronger where I am."

Barney cautiously extended his hand and then jerked it back. "Right. You feel like a cactus."

Tibbo laughed. "I sure do like you, Barney."

"Yeah? How do you know me?"

"I've been watching you for a couple of days and listening to you."

"How? *How?*" Barney was near the end of his patience.

"Hang on, Barney," said Tibbo. "This is going to be hard for you to believe."

"I'm ready."

There was the sound of Tibbo drawing a deep breath.

"You know that silver ball you saw last night? You called it a UFO. Unidentified Flying Object. Well, I can identify that object. That was a space ship and I was in it. I brought that ship down myself. I looked at you standing there on the roof."

"How come I couldn't see you?" asked Barney. "I

45

didn't see any windows in that space ship.''

"The whole ship's a window. I can see out, but no one can see in. Clever, isn't it?''

"Eh!" said Barney, shrugging his shoulders. "Sounds like a one-way mirror, and they're common enough. By the way, that wasn't a very big space ship.''

"Of course not,'' said Tibbo. "That was a piggy-back ship. One of our mini ships. We carry them along for short trips. Our big space ship is several thousand miles above the Earth. In fact, my body's in it now. We're rotating at the same speed as the Earth, so we stay over the same spot.''

"So you didn't come down in that silver ball this time?''

"Right.''

Barney was dazed. There were too many new ideas for him to absorb all at once. Where was Tibbo's home? Had he come from some other country? But what country was so far developed in science that the people could talk from several thousand miles up as if they were in the same room, and see everything in the room, too? Barney was almost afraid to put his question into words, but he had to know.

"Where'd your space ship come from?'' he asked.

"From the planet Ornam.''

It was as Barney had guessed. Tibbo was not an Earth person. "Ornam?'' he said. "I never heard of it.''

"Of course not," replied Tibbo. "It's more than twenty-five trillion miles from Earth."

"Twenty-five trillion!" gasped Barney. He couldn't even imagine a distance that great.

"Yes. Ornam's up there in the Milky Way. One of those stars is our sun."

"It must've taken you a long time to get here."

"Not as long as you might think. We travel almost as fast as the speed of light. That's about 186,000 miles per second."

"Space ships can't go that fast. You're kidding me."

"Not at all, Earth boy. I came here at just under the speed of light, and it didn't take very long."

"Oh." Barney wasn't able to argue the point. He wished Dick were here. He'd know how to answer.

Tibbo said, "I couldn't expect you to know any better. Ornam is thousands of years older than Earth, and we're way past Earth in science and everything else."

Ahead of Earth! Barney was ready to stand up for his own planet. "If Ornam's so great, why'd you come here? How come you're calling on me?"

Tibbo chuckled. "I didn't mean to hurt your feelings, Barney. Earth's a great planet, or we wouldn't be visiting it. And I have a reason for getting acquainted with you. A very good reason." His voice seemed to move away. "Time for me to shove off. I have work to do in the space ship."

"Wait!" cried Barney.

"I can't stay much longer." Tibbo sounded impatient. "I don't want to get in trouble with the Garks again. Believe me, they had a few words to say last night because I brought the mini ship down here."

"The Garks? Who are they?"

"The people who live on Ornam. The grownups, that is. The kids are called—well, in your language it would be Garkins. I'm still a Garkin."

"Oh," said Barney. "How come you can speak English? Is that the language you use on Ornam?"

"Certainly not. I've been studying English all the way here. Besides, I listened to your radio broadcasts, and when we got near enough I watched your TV programs, too. How's my accent?"

"Perfect. I'd think you were an American."

"Thanks. My French and Czechoslovakian aren't bad, either. Well, so long."

"Don't go yet!" Barney wished he could hold Tibbo back, but how could you hang onto someone who wasn't there? "At least tell me about the prickles. What makes them?"

"They come from the power we use when we want to zero in on someone. It's a high frequency wave. You know how your space satellites look down and see what the weather is on Earth and check up on other countries

48

to see if they're making atomic weapons or rockets?''

"Yes."

"What we do is like that, only stronger. When you feel the prickles, you know I'm watching you. I can hear you and see you."

"Can you tell what I'm thinking?"

"Some of the time, but not always." Again his voice had begun to fade.

"Don't go!" Barney was on his knees on the bed. "There's lots more I want—"

But the light had left the room, and Barney's skin no longer tingled.

Bursting with excitement, Barney got up and began to pace the floor.

A boy from outer space! From the planet Ornam! This was even more wonderful than the UFO.

He went to the window, even though he knew he wouldn't see the silver ship tonight.

Several thousand miles up! That was a long way, but satellites orbited at that distance, he had heard, and people saw them.

What about telescopes? They could focus on objects that far away. Why hadn't someone reported a UFO?

Barney went back and sat on the edge of his bed. He began to doubt himself. How could a boy from a planet trillions of miles away talk to him? And in English? Tibbo would have to be awfully smart to have learned to speak so well while he was on the way here. Was someone playing a trick on him? Was there a hidden speaker in the room? But what had made the bundle of sharp prickles when he was sitting next to Tibbo?

50

Strange as it was, he knew it all had really happened.

Slowly Barney walked into the hall and stood in front of the Crandalls' room. In spite of his determination not to talk about his experience, he longed to share it with them. Several times he put out his hand to the door-knob, but he didn't touch it.

He felt more alone than ever before in his life. Again something great and exciting had happened and he had no one with whom he could share it.

He could write to his friend Howie. But would even Howie believe what had happened? If he could talk to him face to face he could make him understand, but going to see him was out of the question. Buffalo was too far from Pineville.

As Barney turned away from the Crandalls' room, he heard a rustle in the hallway.

"Who's that?" he whispered.

Scott's sleepy voice replied, "I have to go to the bathroom."

"All right," said Barney. "Go ahead."

He went back to his own room and lay down. His mind was still racing. He kept thinking of questions he wanted to ask Tibbo. He wondered if he would return. Next time perhaps he would come in the mini space ship. The piggy-back ship. It must be that it was carried by the larger ship in some way, sort of like a lifeboat on an ocean ship.

"Barney." A voice spoke softly, just inside the door of his room.

Barney drew in a quick, startled breath. Was Tibbo back already? A second later he realized it was Scott's voice he had heard.

When he looked toward the door he could see his little brother in the dim light, standing like a small, lost ghost, a ghost with feet in his pajamas.

Barney raised up on one elbow. "What d'you want?"

"Nothing."

"Then go back to bed."

"It's dark. I'm lonesome."

Barney could understand that. He got up again and went over to Scott. "Come on, Tiger."

He took his brother's hand and led him back to his room. It actually wasn't very dark, for a tiny night light shed a glow like moonlight.

The little boy's bed was so full of stuffed animals there wasn't much room for Scott.

It's a regular zoo, thought Barney.

He pushed aside a giraffe and a two-foot high rabbit. "Climb in," he told his brother. As he pulled up the blanket, he noticed that the toy space ship was on the bedside table.

Barney sat down on the edge of the bed and picked up the toy. He ran his hand over the smooth plastic dome.

"There are real space ships something like this," he

52

remarked. He longed to describe Tibbo's silver ship.

Scott yawned. "I know. I saw 'em on TV." Now that he was in bed he looked contented and sleepy.

Barney returned the space ship to the bedside table and tucked the covers around his brother's shoulders.

As he lay in his own bed, Barney felt less alone than before. He still didn't have a person to whom he could talk, but it was good to know someone needed him.

When he awakened the next morning, his first thought was of Tibbo.

While he showered and dressed, he wondered what the space boy was doing. It would be great to see what he looked like. Today, with the sun shining and Finn outside barking at a squirrel, it was hard to believe a boy from Ornam had visited him last night.

I must be the only person in the world who has talked to someone from outer space, he thought as he made his bed. Why am I the lucky one? He recalled one of Tibbo's remarks. "I have a reason for visiting you. A very good reason."

Barney shivered, although the room was warm and sunny. Perhaps he wasn't as lucky as he thought. It depended on Tibbo's reason for talking to him.

He pulled up the corduroy bedspread, glad that it was thick enough to conceal most of the wrinkles underneath.

As he headed for the stairs he told himself that if

Tibbo had plans for him he'd surely come back. And this time Barney hoped he could get the answers to a lot more questions.

8   BARNEY IS A HERO

Barney was mowing the lawn at ten o'clock that morning when Kara walked down the road with her father. Mr. MacDougall went along the driveway to where Mr. Crandall was working on the old car, the one his wife used for short trips, going to Pineville for groceries and things like that. They had a better car, but this one was Mrs. Crandall's pet. She called it George, and Mr. Crandall was always fixing it.

Kara ran across the grass toward Barney. She shouted something, but the power mower was making so much noise Barney couldn't hear a word. He decided the only polite thing to do was shut it off.

"My father!" Kara was still shouting. She laughed and went on in her normal quiet voice. "Thanks for stopping that thing. Dad and I want to go to the game this afternoon. We came over to see if we can ride with you and the Crandalls. Mom's getting her hair done, so she needs the car. We only have one."

"I'm sure Mr. Crandall will give you a lift. Probably in the good car." He nodded over his shoulder. "The old one doesn't want to start this morning—as usual."

Kara smiled. She knew about the old car. "I'm really looking forward to seeing the game," she said softly.

Barney grinned self-consciously. "Here's hoping you aren't expecting to see any big league action. This is the Patriots' first game. I'll be going over early on my bike. I'll see you there."

"Dad will have a good time, no matter how the game turns out. My mother says he'd rather watch baseball than eat. He's a good player," said Kara proudly. "He used to play pro ball a long time ago."

When Barney arrived at the diamond behind the Pineville Volunteer Firehall, a few other players were already there, warming up for the game. Three of the boys were from his class.

As soon as he parked his bike, one of his classmates shouted, "Come on over! Here's Dick's glove."

It felt good to be handling a softball again. Barney was filled with new happiness. So far today he hadn't noticed a single prickle on his skin. That in itself was enough to make him feel better. However, he didn't think the tingling would bother him as much as before, now that he knew what caused it. The worst of the prickles had been thinking that he had some kind of sickness.

56

He put all thoughts of Tibbo out of his mind while he concentrated on throwing and catching. Every now and then he missed the ball. He was out of practice, that was sure, and it would take him a while to get back into the swing.

In a few minutes he had a chance for a little batting practice.

The team from Valmora arrived in four cars driven by parents. Barney sized up the opponents. They looked about the same age as the Pineville Patriots, and they didn't appear to live up to their fierce name of Vultures.

He noticed that the parents were beginning to gather on benches over to the side. Some of the students from his school were there, too. The Crandalls, Scott, and Kara and her father were in a row on one of the benches. Scott stood up and waved to him. Barney waved back and then missed the next ball that was thrown to him. He felt as if he were on stage and didn't know his lines.

The Valmora Vultures, being the visitors, were up to bat first. As Barney trotted out to right field, he hoped that he wouldn't miss any balls. With all those people watching, he felt nervous.

At the start the two teams seemed to be quite evenly matched, but before long the Valmora team edged ahead.

Barney put everything he had into the game. In the

first half of the second inning he caught a fly. When he came up to bat in the last half of the inning he hit a foul ball on the first pitch. On the second pitch he whacked a grounder that allowed him to reach first base. The next player struck out, making the third out for the Pineville Patriots after a scoreless inning for them.

When Barney started back to the field, Jake came up to him. "You're okay," he said. "How about joining the team?"

Barney nodded happily. "Great!" A whole summer of ball! Not only that, he'd make some new friends.

His luck failed him in the third inning and he missed an easy fly ball.

Gloom settled over him like a cloud.

There goes my chance for the team, he thought. But Jake said nothing.

The score was now 3–0 in favor of the Vultures.

The Crandalls must be disappointed, Barney thought. But when he looked their way, they waved as enthusiastically as ever.

When it was his turn to bat in the fourth inning, Barney was discouraged before he went up to the plate.

Two players were already out and a runner was on second. Barney knew a lot depended on him. A good hit could put the Patriots on the scoreboard, but he was afraid he wasn't the one who could deliver. He was tired and he was sure he'd strike out again.

His hands felt slippery no matter how he rubbed them on the sides of his jeans.

"Come on, Barney!" he heard someone shout.

He went to the plate and lifted his bat. At that moment he felt a tingle all over his skin. Tibbo had come to the game! Now Barney feared he'd really make a mess of it. He gritted his teeth, determined to give it his all.

"Get lost, Tibbo!" he muttered.

The ball came toward him, over the plate but a little low.

"Ball one!" called the umpire.

Barney was glad he hadn't swung at that one. He braced himself for the next pitch. Now the prickles were worse than ever.

The ball came toward him, a good one. Barney swung and connected. He dropped the bat and ran.

The crowd was shouting, and as Barney touched first base and took a quick glance to see where the ball was, he wondered why people were so excited. He hadn't heard such a roar since the game started.

A voice separated itself from the general shouting.

"Keep going!" That was Jake.

Barney headed for second. Still the ball had not returned. He kept on running, touched third, and made it back home.

His entire team rushed toward him, slapping him on the back, yelling, wild with excitement.

"A home run!" shouted one of his classmates. "I never saw a hit like that!"

"You knocked it clean out of the field!" cried another.

When there was an opening in the crowd around him, Barney glimpsed Mr. Crandall. He was standing on the bench and holding Scott high in the air over his head. Both had their mouths wide open. They must be cheering.

Barney was dazed. He had never sent a ball that far before. It hadn't felt like a great hit. He looked at the board where the scorekeeper had changed the Patriots' score from zero to two. They had made two runs on his hit.

Jake came over to him. "Why didn't you tell me you were a champion hitter?" He sounded almost angry.

"I'm not," said Barney. "That was luck."

Jake shook his head. He had lost his cap in the excitement and his black hair was standing on end. "That wasn't luck. You've got power. They're still looking for the ball."

Just then a Valmora fielder, far outside the diamond in a grassy lot, held up the ball.

"Look where you sent it," said Jake. "Hit another like that next time and we may take this game."

There's something funny about this, thought Barney

as he went back to the bench to watch the next batter. He knew for certain he couldn't hit a ball as far as that one had gone. Was it possible Tibbo could have helped?

The Patriot batter struck out and the inning was over.

Neither team scored in the fifth and sixth innings, and the Valmora team had no runs in the first half of the seventh.

When Barney came up to bat in the second half of the inning, the score was still 3–2 in favor of the Vultures. The Patriots already had two outs. One player was on third, but the other bases were empty. The supporters of the Patriots were shouting, "You can do it, Barney!" "We're counting on you!" "Yea, Barney!"

It gave Barney a warm feeling to hear them. He no longer felt the tingle that told him Tibbo was watching. Whatever he did now, he'd be doing it on his own.

With the first pitch, he hit a long ground ball. A Vulture fielder grabbed the ball and then overthrew it to the first baseman. While the Vulture supporters groaned, the man on third reached home and Barney sped on to second base.

The score was tied at 3–3.

The batter that followed hit a two-bagger, giving Barney time to scramble home from second. The Patriots had won, 4–3.

When some of the excitement had died down, Jake

came up to Barney. "Thanks a lot. We wouldn't have made it without you. Can you come to practice Monday at ten?"

"Sure. But don't get your hopes up. I'm not usually this good."

"Okay," Jake agreed. "We all have our days. But I like the way you handle the ball. And bat."

Mr. MacDougall, Kara's father, came over to shake Barney's hand. "Best hit I ever saw outside the big leagues." He turned to Jake. "Do you kids have a coach?"

"No, sir," answered Jake. "We've looked for one, but no one has time to work with us."

"I'll find the time if you want me," said Mr. Mac-Dougall. "I've played quite a lot and I umpire now and then. You have a good team started and you deserve some help."

"I'll ask the other kids and let you know right away." Jake's eyes were shining. "I know what they'll say."

When Mr. MacDougall had gone, Jake said, "I've heard he knows the game inside out. Are we ever in luck! We're going to have a great team, Barney!"

9 ☙☙☙ TROUBLE

The crowd was beginning to thin.

Mr. Crandall came over to Barney and put his hand on his shoulder.

"Nice work, Barney," he said. "I wouldn't have missed it for anything."

Barney felt embarrassed and uncomfortable. He was quite sure he was getting more credit than he deserved. He wanted to mention the possibility that Tibbo had given the ball an extra push, but he couldn't do that unless he was ready to tell about the UFO and Tibbo's night visit.

"I don't know how I happened to hit that home run," he said. "I'm not that good a hitter."

"It wasn't just the run," said Mr. Crandall. "That was amazing. But you look to me like a good, solid player. I like the way you handle yourself on the field. You pay attention to your job. You don't have your eye on the crowd, trying to make a grandstand play."

Mrs. Crandall, with Scott beside her, joined them.

Her face was pink with sun and the excitement of the game. "It was just great!" she said enthusiastically.

"Great!" echoed Scott.

"Thank you," said Barney gravely. "I'll get my bike now and see you at home."

He was taking his bicycle from the rack when Kara ran up to him. "Want me to ride your bike home?" she offered. "Then you could go with your family. Maybe you're tired after the game. It was terrific!"

"Thanks," said Barney. "But I'd really like to ride home myself." He wanted time alone to think about the afternoon. It was nice of Kara to offer, though. She was the kind of girl he might like to date in a couple of years.

He started down the road, buoyed up by his success and the praise he had received. He was glad Mr. Crandall had liked his playing as a whole, and not just that hit. Pedaling the bike was no effort. He seemed to float along, propelled by happiness.

Half a block from the firehall, another member of the Pineville team caught up with him on his bike. Barney didn't know his name, but everyone called him Rabbit.

The boy fell into place beside Barney. "Hi. Are you the kid who lives with the Crandalls?"

"Yes. I'm Barney Galloway. Why?"

"No reason. My mother knows Mrs. Crandall. Sorta. She has a friend who's a friend of hers."

"Oh."

Rabbit dropped behind Barney as a car approached. Once the road was clear he again eased up beside him.

"My mom thought it was funny the Crandalls took a kid your age. She heard they were looking for a little kid."

Barney pedaled in silence. He felt as if he were going to be sick.

Rabbit went on. "Guess you must be doing all right. They were both there to watch you play and all."

"Yeah," said Barney. It was the only thing he could think of to say. He wished Rabbit would go away and leave him alone.

"Who's the little guy with them?" asked Rabbit.

"My brother."

"Oh, so that's it."

"What do you mean by that?" Barney turned his head and met Rabbit's eyes, staring at him with open curiosity.

Rabbit looked away. "Nothing. Well, so long. This is where I turn off." He went up a side street. Before he was out of earshot he called back, "See you Monday."

Barney continued in a daze. Rabbit had wiped out the joy he had felt only moments ago.

So the Crandalls were like all of the others who were looking for someone to adopt. They, too, wanted a young child. This must be what the boy at the orphanage had heard.

He said I'd be back, thought Barney. Maybe I will.

The appearance of a car directly in his path startled him out of his dark thoughts. The orange sports car, which had been parked at the curb, had started to pull out just as Barney was passing it. The boy made a quick, wide swing to the left to avoid running into the side of the vehicle. A second later he heard the screeching of brakes.

Barney glanced around and saw a large blue car with its bumper against a lamppost on the opposite side of the street.

That car must have been behind him, he thought. Probably the driver swerved to avoid hitting him and his bicycle. Only he swerved too far. Lucky for him there hadn't been any cars in the way.

Barney pulled over to the right and stopped. Traffic had now come to a halt in the oncoming lane. The driver had gotten out and started toward the front of his car, but before he reached the bumper, his eyes fastened on Barney.

Raising his clenched fist, he shouted angrily, "You come back here!"

For one terrified moment Barney stared at the red-faced man. Then, instead of going back, he thrust his feet onto the pedals and poured on the speed. He skidded around the next corner, narrowly missing a young woman with a baby carriage. Up the street he went as fast as he could go.

A cross street went off to the right but he ignored

that. The road he was on soon bore left across a bridge, and suddenly he was in the country north of Pineville. No houses were in sight, and thick bushes bordered the road which began a steep climb up a hill.

Barney leaped to the ground and forced his way into the bushes, pulling his bike with him. Immediately he and the bicycle were out of sight of the road. There he stayed for almost half an hour, fighting the mosquitoes and watching through the branches, expecting at any time to see the blue car roaring across the bridge with an angry man at the wheel.

He tried to reason with himself. That man couldn't have followed him. First he had to back away from that lamppost, and if he had damaged it, he might've had to report to the police. Unconvinced, Barney continued to wait.

Only a small foreign car went past. Finally Barney crept out of his hiding place. The man must have given up and gone home by now. But just in case he was still waiting, Barney stuffed his red cap inside his shirt. He had been wearing that at the time of the accident. Perhaps the man wouldn't recognize him without it.

In order to reach his own road south of Pineville, Barney had to cross the main street of the town. As he made the crossing, he figured he came as close as a bicyclist could to the speed of light.

All the way home, every time he heard a car approaching, Barney worried until it passed him and he

67

could see it was not the dreaded blue car. He knew that whenever he went to Pineville he was going to be afraid of meeting that man.

Why had he run away? he asked himself. His father had always told him it was better to stay and face up to things. He remembered having to go to a neighbor once to confess that he was the one who had stepped on the wet cement of a new driveway. And once he had taken an apple from a fruit stand. He had had to pay for that from his own allowance.

When he thought about it, he knew why he had run this time, even though he hadn't done anything wrong intentionally. It was because he didn't want to get into any trouble that would make the Crandalls send him back to the orphanage. Now, probably, he had done the worst possible thing. What if the man had recognized him? It seemed that everyone in Pineville knew everyone else.

Suddenly a picture flashed across his memory. That car, that same blue car, had been parked at the ball field. Its owner must have been watching the game. He'd have no trouble at all finding out the name of the boy with the red cap. Everyone would know the kid who hit the home run.

The fine bike that Mr. Crandall had bought him had never seemed so hard to pump.

Barney's mind returned to Rabbit's remarks. He had

no doubt that the boy was telling the truth. Why would a young couple like the Crandalls want a boy as old as he? They must have taken him because it was the only way they could get Scott.

That hurt Barney's pride. He wanted to be chosen for himself.

He put his bike into the garage and took his cap out of his shirt. He wished he could crawl up to his room and not even have to eat dinner.

He opened the back door and started up the steps. Suddenly the door at the head of the stairs flew open and the air vibrated with the sound of a trumpet playing a familiar tune. In a second Barney recognized "Take Me Out to the Ball Game."

Mr. Crandall appeared in the doorway with the trumpet at his lips, still playing. When Barney, laughing in spite of himself, came up the steps, Mr. Crandall turned around and marched through the kitchen followed by Scott and Mrs. Crandall. They motioned Barney to fall in line.

All through the house they went, upstairs and down, with Mrs. Crandall singing and Scott giggling and trying to sing. Barney brought up the rear, red with embarrassment, but enjoying himself, too. Perhaps Rabbit was wrong. If the Crandalls didn't want him why were they making such a fuss over him?

Finn McCool ran in and out between the marchers

with his mouth open as if he were laughing.

Mr. and Mrs. MacDougall and Kara came over that night in time for dessert. Again Barney was surprised when Mrs. Crandall brought out a cake decorated with a ball and bat and with his name written across the top. There were four candles on it.

"It isn't my birthday," Barney protested when the cake was set in front of him. "And I'm a lot more than four!"

"But your team had four runs today," said Kara.

"That's what I had in mind," agreed Mrs. Crandall. "This was a hurry-up job," she confessed. "I made the cake before we went to the game. I didn't have any idea of a celebration then. When we got home, I decided we had to have a party, so I decorated it in a hurry."

They had eaten their ice cream and slices of cake and were sitting around the table talking when the phone rang. Mr. Crandall went into the living room to answer it. He was gone for several minutes and Barney began to feel uneasy.

When his foster father returned to the table he acted the same as usual, talking and making a joke now and then.

It was only after the guests had gone that he came upstairs and joined Barney in his bedroom. As Barney had guessed, the call had been from the red-faced driver who had ended up on the wrong side of the street be-

70

cause of him. His name was Mr. Jardine.

Mr. Crandall was worried about Barney's safety on the bike, he said, but even more concerned because he had run away. "I've always thought you were a person who faced up to trouble."

Barney said nothing. How could he explain why he had run this time?

Mr. Crandall got to his feet. "One more thing. The two drivers were at fault, too. The first one should have looked more carefully before he drove out. But that's something a good bicyclist has to watch out for. And if Mr. Jardine had been going more slowly, he wouldn't have lost control of his car."

When Barney was alone in his room he did not move from his place on the edge of the bed. Mr. Crandall had been fair. He had talked to him like a real father.

But Barney's spirits had hit a new low. Who would want to adopt a kid who would run and hide, who was too chicken to face up to what he had done?

He took a long time getting ready for bed. Even when he was in his pajamas, he picked up a mystery and read for an hour.

Finally he closed the book. Nothing he read seemed as exciting and hard to figure out as his own life.

The Crandalls were in their room when he went down the hall to the bathroom. He could hear them walking around and talking. As he passed their room on his way back, Mr. Crandall's steps sounded near the door and his voice came clearly to Barney.

"And I say it's time to get rid of him!"

Barney's heart leaped into his throat.

Then Mrs. Crandall answered, her voice less plain. "Have you no heart?"

Barney continued blindly down the hall. They were talking about him! This was the end. He had really blown it when he ran away from Mr. Jardine.

He went into his room, turned off the light, and sat on the bed, numb with grief.

How *could* Mr. Crandall act so kind and then turn around and say it was time to get rid of him?

I never thought he was two-faced, mourned Barney. If he's like that, how can I believe in anybody?

He was still sitting on the bed when he heard the click of Finn McCool's toenails on the stairs. A moment later the dog padded into the room and jumped up beside his master.

Barney's arms closed fiercely around him. "At least *you* like me," he whispered. "You'll miss me when I get sent away."

When he went to bed, Finn lay against his feet, and although the dog was supposed to sleep in the kitchen, Barney couldn't bear to give up his company tonight.

10 ₩₩₩ TIBBO COMES AGAIN

"Barney! Come out!"

As soon as Tibbo spoke that night, Barney was wide awake and eager to talk. After the problems of the past day, it would be a relief to have a visitor from another world.

He sat up on the edge of the bed and looked toward the window. The voice had come from that direction.

Two short steps took Barney to the window. There was no moon, but the meadow behind the house was covered with the same shining mist he had seen on the night of the UFO.

"Tibbo!" Barney called softly. "Where are you?"

"Here!" The voice came from the mist-covered lawn below the window. "Come on down!"

Barney hesitated for only a moment. "Right away," he agreed. This time he'd go by the stairs.

Tibbo would make sure no one heard him.

He started toward the chest of drawers to get a

sweater, but as he passed the foot of his bed, there was Finn, lying perfectly still.

Barney's heart missed a beat. He stopped and put his hand on the dog's side. The even rise and fall of his breathing was reassuring, but why didn't he wake up?

Barney ran back to the window. "What'd you do to my dog?"

Tibbo's voice sounded impatient. "He's all right. He's just sleeping. You don't want him to start barking, do you?"

"What does it matter, as long as you soundproofed the rooms?"

"Oh, come on! I don't have all night."

Barney checked Finn once more. Then he pulled on a sweater over his pajama top and slid his bare feet into his sneakers.

When he let himself out the back door, he took off the night lock. No sense in getting locked out. He'd have trouble explaining that.

As soon as he reached the porch, electricity seemed to dance on his face and bare hands.

"Isn't this a super night?" asked Tibbo at his elbow. "That meadow. The way the mist shines, you'd think it was snow."

"I bet you had something to do with it," said Barney. "And the night the UFO came, too. This kind of mist doesn't look like anything I've ever seen. I keep

74

thinking a Gark will come walking out of it.''

"Don't talk to me about Garks," said Tibbo sulkily. "They made me spend the day cleaning up the ship."

"Tough," Barney teased him. "If you think you have it hard you should be in my shoes." Then he pushed his troubles out of his mind. "Why did you come to see me?" he asked.

For once Tibbo was willing to be serious. "Because I'm lonesome. I'm the only Garkin on this trip and I don't have anyone to play with or talk to. It has been even worse since we reached Earth because most of the Garks go off on missions."

Barney interrupted. "I suppose they use that silver ball you brought down here the other night."

"Right," said Tibbo. "They leave me alone to look after the big ship. That's how I happened to find you. One day I got bored so I sat down at the earth scanner. I saw you get off the school bus and walk down the road all alone."

"That's when I got the feeling like electricity in the air."

"Does it bother you?"

"Some," admitted Barney. "But not as much now that I know what causes it. By the way, did you help me make that home run yesterday?"

"Me? Hit a home run? How could I do that?" Tibbo had laughter in his voice.

"You could if you wanted to, I bet."

"I'll have to try sometime," said Tibbo lightly.

Barney could see he wasn't going to get a straight answer, so he tried another question. "The first time you came you said you had a reason for getting acquainted with me. What reason?"

"You're an orphan."

"What difference does that make?"

Tibbo did not explain. Instead he remarked, "Parents and children don't stay together on Ornam, but we've noticed the family's a big thing on Earth. The father and mother protect the children like tigers. The children fight with each other, yet if any outsider bothers one of them, they all pitch into him."

"Yeah, that's right," agreed Barney. "Don't you have any families on Ornam?"

"In a way we do. I have a father and mother, but as soon as I was born they took me to a big nursery. We have Garks who are specially trained to raise children. My parents are specialists in growing food. What do they know about raising children?"

Barney shrugged. "On Earth if you have a baby, you raise it. I liked having parents. I wish mine were alive now." For a moment he dared to think back. "It was great having someone who really cared what happened to me. And at Christmas I'd make the dumbest potholders and stuff like that, and they always turned out to be just what my mom and dad wanted."

Tibbo sounded wistful. "It does sound good." Barney felt the prickles become sharper as Tibbo moved nearer. "But I want to tell you about Ornam. Barney, you can't imagine what fun it is to live there! We don't have any schools, not like you do. We all work as soon as we're able, and we learn while we work. My specialty is space travel. That's why I was chosen for this trip."

"I don't think I'd want to go to work yet," said Barney.

"You'd like it. You'd choose something you like to do. It's the best kind of play." With a lightning-fast change of subject, Tibbo suggested, "Let's go out in the meadow."

Barney looked down at his pajama-clad legs. "It'll be all wet with that mist."

"Oh, come on. You aren't afraid of a little water, are you?"

There was no arguing with Tibbo. "All right," agreed Barney. "But it isn't fair. You won't get wet."

Tibbo chuckled. "Come on!" Already his voice came from the edge of the meadow.

Walking through the mist was a strange sensation. It reached as high as Barney's armpits, and when he looked down he couldn't see his body at all. He seemed to be walking through a radiant cloud that rolled like a sea and sent up sprays of light.

He began to run and to toss the mist into the air with

his hands. It felt great—like balls of delicate prickles.

Tibbo circled around him. "Keep it up, Barney! Oh, I wish I could do that, too. I'm tired of being cooped up."

Finally Barney stopped for lack of breath. He could feel the porcupine prickle of Tibbo close beside him.

"Barney, I want to tell you why our space ships are here."

"There's more than one?"

"Yes, there are several, spread out all around Earth."

"How do they keep out of sight?"

"We know how to fool your radar, and your telescopes, too." Tibbo sounded amused. "Once in a while someone sees one of our ships and reports a UFO, but not many people believe it."

"But why are you here?" asked Barney.

Tibbo's voice sounded older than usual when he answered. "Ornam is in trouble. Our sun is getting too hot. That's what happens when a sun gets old and begins to die."

The mist had dropped lower. Now it was only knee high.

Barney began to walk slowly back toward the house. "That's funny. You'd think a dying sun would get cold."

"That's not the way it works. First it gets hotter. In three or four thousand years our sun will be so hot we'll

80

have to move to new planets. Maybe one of them will be Earth.''

"I don't think there's room for many Garks here," said Barney doubtfully. "I'm sure there won't be by then."

"We could help you work that out," Tibbo assured him. "We could teach you to use the oceans better and how to grow food in less space. In three thousand years your Earthmen will be wiser, too."

"I'm afraid you're in for a fight," Barney warned. "In the United States we don't even have any immigration quotas for people from other planets."

Tibbo said gravely, "We know the Earth is warlike. That's why we don't land here. We're peaceful, and we don't want any trouble. But we're picking up people to take back to Ornam with us. We'll teach them and then bring them back to Earth. They can prepare the way for us."

Barney shivered. Suddenly he was afraid. "How do you get the people?"

"Well, the Garks rescue people who are drowning in the sea or catch those who are falling in airplanes. Things like that."

"They've done this before?"

"Yes. For years."

"Then people who disappear, like in the Bermuda Triangle—the Garks have them?"

"Sometimes."

"Wow!" That was really exciting, thought Barney. Lots of people that everyone was sure were dead were alive on Ornam. "Have you ever brought back any of the people you've picked up?"

"Not yet. We will someday when the time is right."

"You ought to bring them back now," objected Barney. "The people on Earth think they're dead."

"They're in no hurry to come back," said Tibbo. "They like life on Ornam."

"But how do people from the Earth breathe?"

"That's the great thing. On Ornam we breathe oxygen, just as you do."

"What do they eat?"

"Our food's different, but the Earth people like it. And we look a lot like you, too. Of course I think we're more handsome," said Tibbo smugly.

"Yeah," said Barney. "You with your green skin and three eyes."

"Wrong on both counts," said Tibbo, laughing. He seemed to get excited when he talked about his home. His voice moved up and down as if he were dancing in the air. "No one's poor. Anyone who wants to can take a vacation at the seashore or in the mountains."

Barney said wistfully, "I wish I could see you. And I'd like to see Ornam, too."

They had reached the old stone wall that ran the length of the meadow.

Tibbo said, "Sit down a minute."

Barney sat on the wall and jumped up again quickly. "The stone's cold. I'm cold, too, with all this mist."

"I'll take care of that," offered Tibbo. "Now try it."

Barney obeyed. This time the rock felt like a heated cushion. Warm air folded itself around him like a blanket.

"Thanks," said Barney. "You're a magician."

"No magic. Just science." Tibbo was close beside him. "Barney, you said you'd like to see Ornam. Did you mean that?"

"Of course. Anybody'd want to take a trip on a space ship and see a wonderful planet like Ornam." It would be even better than going to the moon, he thought. And when he came back to Earth he'd really have something to tell Dick and the kids at school—if he were still living here.

The mist in front of Barney spun like a small tornado. From the middle of the whirling column came Tibbo's eager voice.

"You can, Barney! Our space ships are going home in a few days. Come back with me!"

11 ᛝᛝᛝ THE SKELETON BARN

The small tornado of mist in front of Barney rose into the air and disappeared. Had Tibbo gone with it? His words still echoed in Barney's ears. "Come back with me!"

Was it possible? Could he really go to Ornam? It would be great to get away from Mr. Jardine and all of his other problems.

"How about it?" Tibbo's voice surprised Barney. It came from the air in front of him. "Will you go?"

"I'd like to. But let me think about it. What would the Garks say?"

"That's all taken care of," said Tibbo. Now he spoke from the stone wall beside Barney. "You know I said I was especially interested because you were an orphan?"

"Yes, I remember."

"That's what makes it so perfect," said Tibbo. "The Garks said I could take a friend back with me, but it couldn't be anyone who had strong ties on Earth."

"What about those people you snatch from drowning

and things like that? Some of them have parents.''

"It's different with them,'' explained Tibbo. "They'd be dead if we didn't rescue them. We give them a whole new life and they like it. In your case, you'd be going of your own free will—and if you don't have a family, nobody'll get upset.''

"There are the Crandalls,'' said Barney slowly. "But I guess they wouldn't mind.'' He turned toward the place where he thought Tibbo was. "I got in a lot of trouble yesterday, and I found out that the Crandalls don't want me.''

Tibbo cut in. "See, you're the right one to go. And I like you.''

Barney wanted to be completely honest with Tibbo. "The Crandalls still might not want me to go to Ornam.''

"Don't worry about it,'' said Tibbo. "As long as you're an orphan, it's okay with the Garks. Barney, we're going to have a lot of fun together. Wait till you see the Earth from space. It's a huge blue ball with cloud feathers wrapped around it. It looks like—like one of those marbles you kids play with. Agates. Aggies, you call them.''

Barney was still trying to decide if he should go. "There's Scott,'' he said, thinking out loud. "He'd miss me while I was gone, but he'd be all right with the Crandalls.''

"So that's settled," said Tibbo. "You'll go!"

It was a big decision. He wondered if the Garks really knew Tibbo was planning to take him to Ornam. Sometimes it seemed as if the space boy would say anything to get what he wanted.

Well, decided Barney, it was worth taking a chance to go on that wonderful ride through space. When he came back, maybe the Crandalls would want to keep a boy who had traveled even farther than the astronauts.

"I'll go," answered Barney.

Tibbo replied solemnly, "You'll never regret—"

His voice broke off abruptly. At the same time Barney's skin stopped prickling. Why had Tibbo gone so suddenly?

The rock wall was again hard and cold, and the blanket of warm air no longer surrounded Barney. He jumped to the ground and started back toward the house. The mist had vanished as quickly as Tibbo.

Barney had gone only a few steps when the tingling of his skin announced Tibbo's presence. The space boy's voice came to him as if from far away.

"I had a call from one of our mini ships," he said. "There's a storm in the Atlantic and a small fishing boat has turned over. Two men are in the water. They have life jackets on, but some sharks are beginning to take an interest in them."

"Will the Garks save them?" asked Barney.

"Hold on. I'm getting another message."

Barney waited, shivering in the cool air and thinking about the frightened men in the ocean.

Tibbo's voice returned. "They've done it! The Garks have pulled them out of the water. They're taking them to one of our space ships that's stationed over Florida."

"That's great!" exclaimed Barney. "Tibbo, what would happen if our Air Force spotted your mini ship? What would the Garks do if our planes surrounded it?"

"That wouldn't happen," Tibbo said confidently. Again he seemed near to Barney. "Our space ships are a lot faster than your fastest jets."

"Okay. But if our planes were all around your space ship, how would it get away without shooting its way out?"

"I told you, we're peaceful," Tibbo said. "We wouldn't use arms against Earth people."

"Maybe our planes would fire on your ship."

"They couldn't hurt us. Barney, you don't understand. We have powers you Earthmen have never thought of."

Barney taunted him. "That's what you say."

"You don't believe me?" Tibbo's voice was stern. "Then turn around."

Barney obeyed.

"Now," said Tibbo. "Keep your eyes on that barn."

The old barn stood dark and solid in the field, a short distance away. Barney could see its roof gleaming under the stars.

As if in slow motion, the scene began to change. The walls of the barn fell away. The roof boards sailed out like glider planes and clattered to the grass on either side of the crumbling building.

At the same time the air was filled with a cloud of small flying objects. At first Barney thought they were bats, but when they, too, rained to the ground, he knew they must be shingles.

In two or three minutes only the framework remained standing. Under the white light of the stars stood a skeleton barn.

Barney drew a shuddering breath. "You win. You just saved Mr. Crandall a lot of trouble. He was going to take it down this summer."

Suddenly he felt the cold of his mist-wet pajamas. Tibbo had proved that he was not just bragging when he said the Garks had great powers. It was frightening to know that beings with such strong and mysterious forces were even now hovering above the Earth. Barney was glad that they were friendly.

12 🐾🐾🐾 HOW FAR TO ORNAM?

The next morning Finn McCool awakened Barney with a cold nose against his face. He was as frisky as ever and no one complained because he had not slept in his bed in the kitchen.

Barney managed to dry his pajamas in the drier before breakfast while Mrs. Crandall was taking a shower. She discovered his wet sneakers, however, when Finn dragged one of them downstairs and happily chewed it in the living room.

"There was a mist last night," Barney explained. "I was outdoors for a while."

To his relief she said only, "Oh, I didn't know you were out. Well, put them in the sun to dry."

Everything seemed unreal today. On Sunday morning Mr. Crandall always prepared pancakes. They were good, as usual, and in spite of his worries, Barney enjoyed them, scooting the last bite around with his fork to soak up every drop of syrup.

He wondered if there were pancakes on Ornam.

Even while he ate, he felt as if he were looking down on the group in the kitchen from some place high above, as Tibbo did.

He no longer belonged here. No matter how kind the Crandalls were, he now knew they didn't want him. Well, he'd soon be out of the way. In a short time, any day now, he'd be flying off with Tibbo and it might be several months before he'd be back. He hadn't found out how long it would take to get to Ornam or how soon he would be able to return to Earth. He'd ask Tibbo the next time he came.

So far no one had noticed that the barn was down. The old building could not be seen from the master bedroom or the kitchen.

At ten o'clock Barney was in the side yard on the east side of the house with Mrs. Crandall, trimming the grass around the trees and along the driveway. Scott was playing with Finn, letting the dog set his teeth into an old towel and then pulling him around by the towel. Finn seemed to think this was great fun.

Mr. Crandall came down the driveway dressed in his oldest clothes. "George and I are going to have a little conference," he said. "That doggone car still doesn't want to run right."

You'd think that old car was a person, thought Barney, the way the Crandalls talked about it.

His foster father passed the end of the house and

came to a sudden halt. "Will you look at that!" he exclaimed. "Lois!" he called to his wife. "The old barn's down."

"What d'you mean, down?" she asked as she hurried toward him, clippers in hand. "It was all right yester—" Then she, too, saw the naked framework of the barn. "For heaven's sake!"

Barney stopped clipping the grass and strolled into the back yard where his foster parents were standing.

Scott stopped his play long enough for a quick look at the remains of the barn. Then Finn yanked the old towel out of his hands and the little boy ran after him, squealing and laughing.

Mr. Crandall was staring across the meadow with a puzzled expression on his face. "I was out there about a week ago looking it over, and it seemed strong enough. Why would it go down all at once? There wasn't even a wind last night."

"That's right, there wasn't!" Mrs. Crandall agreed. "It's so *flat,* except for the framework. You'd think a barn like that would fall apart a little at a time. First the roof would cave in, and so on."

"Well, whatever, it's down," said her husband. "But I'm going to ask the state police if they've noticed anyone loitering around the place. I just don't see why it would go down like that without some outside help."

"Anyway, now you and Barney don't have to pull it

down," Mrs. Crandall remarked. "And I don't have to worry about anyone's getting hurt on it."

The man sighed. "I'd like to go out right now and see if any of the boards are good enough for your paneling idea, but I'd better not. If I don't get busy with that car, you'll be minus your wheels tomorrow, hon."

Barney went back to trimming the grass.

I could tell you what happened, he thought. *But you'd never believe me.*

Scott, apparently tired of the game with Finn, came running up, clutching his rubber ball. "Show me how to make a home run," he begged.

"When I'm finished with the grass," said Barney.

Mr. Crandall tore his eyes away from the fallen barn. "Go ahead. We can work on that anytime."

Barney put the clippers away in the tool shed. "Get your bat," he told Scott.

Patiently he showed his brother how to hold the little plastic bat. Then he aimed the ball, which was slightly larger than a softball, directly at it. Sometimes bat and ball connected. Oftener they didn't.

"Hey, Tibbo," Barney murmured to himself. "How about giving us some baseball magic now."

But Barney did not feel an answering prickle of his skin, and Scott went on missing.

Finn McCool watched each pitch with bright eyes. Then, like a four-footed fielder, he would dash after the

94

ball. But it was too large for his mouth. Again and again his teeth slid off the smooth rubber until Scott would catch up with him and take the ball away.

Usually Barney would have been bored with the game in a few minutes. But today he watched his brother with new interest. Every time Scott swung and missed, the little boy laughed, tossed down the bat, and chased Finn and the ball. It was going to be a long time before he was a ballplayer, but at least he was willing to try. It would be fun to teach a kid who was that eager. Barney wondered if he'd be there to work with him.

Someone called, ''Barney!''

Barney ran around the end of the house and looked toward the road. It was Dick on his bicycle.

As Barney ran to meet him, he thought he had never been so glad to see anyone.

''I knew you lived down this way, but I wasn't sure exactly where,'' said Dick. ''That your dog?''

''Yeah. That's Finn McCool. And here comes my kid brother.''

Scott shifted his bat to his left hand so he could hold out his right as he had been taught.

''Hey, you're okay,'' said Dick, shaking the small hand. ''You're a ballplayer, I see.''

Scott shrugged and looked shy. ''Except I can't hit the ball.''

''Give it time,'' said Dick. ''Hey, Barney, how about

95

getting your bike and riding around?''

"Great. Come on and meet Mr. and Mrs. Crandall. I'll have to ask if I can leave now.''

The Crandalls seemed to like Dick. "Sure. Go ahead,'' they agreed.

"Me, too?'' asked Scott.

"In about seven years,'' Mrs. Crandall answered with a laugh. She held out her hand. "Let's go in and I'll read you a story.''

Barney and Dick started down the road at a snail's pace, riding side by side. They went in the direction Barney took to get the school bus.

"I hear you won the game for the Patriots,'' remarked Dick. "Everyone's talking about that sensational hit you made.''

"It wasn't all that much,'' said Barney.

Dick chuckled. "Don't hand me that modest act. I wish I'd been there to see it. No kidding, Barney. I've been getting a lot of credit for spotting a winner when I got you to fill in for me.''

"Sure, sure.'' Barney wanted to drop the subject.

"Before I forget it,'' said Dick, "practice is changed to three o'clock on Monday afternoon so Mr. Mac-Dougall can be there. It's all settled. He's going to coach us.''

"Great,'' said Barney. There was just one thing he wanted to talk about with Dick but he couldn't seem to

96

get out the words. To have something to say, he asked, "Did you have a good time in Albany?"

"It was all right." Dick pedaled more slowly. "When we were eating lunch last Thursday you asked me if the air ever felt funny to me. Any special reason you asked that?"

"Yes." Barney still hesitated. Dick would probably think he was a kook.

"Yes, what?"

Barney clutched his handlebars. "The air feels prickly sometimes, like needles."

"I never noticed anything like that," Dick said flatly.

Though he was disappointed, it was what Barney had expected. He continued, "That's not all. Since I was talking to you, I saw a UFO."

"You did!" Dick looked at Barney with blue eyes that blazed with excitement. "When?"

"Thursday night."

"What'd it look like?"

"Like a big silver ball with a ring around it."

Dick stopped his bike. "Let's get off and talk."

They had traveled so slowly they had gone only a few hundred feet.

Barney pointed to the stone wall in the meadow. "Want to go up there?"

The boys wheeled their bicycles off the road and laid them on the grass.

In silence they walked up the easy slope with last year's dried weeds whipping their ankles. Once they roused a chunky brown meadowlark that popped out of the grass with a startled song and flew away showing a flash of white on the outer edges of its short tail.

They followed the wall back toward Crandalls' house until they found a section that was level and solid enough to hold them. Two hundred feet behind them was the flattened barn.

Dick nodded toward the barn. "When did that happen? Last time I was down this way it was all in one piece."

"That's part of what I want to tell you."

Dick settled down on the stone wall. "Let's have it. Don't leave out anything."

Barney began to talk. It was such a relief to share his experience with someone that the words poured out. He told about the sparkling mist and exactly how the UFO had looked and even why he had not told the Crandalls or anyone else what he had seen. So Dick would understand his adoption problems, he repeated what Rabbit had told him and how he heard Mr. Crandall saying, "It's time to get rid of him."

The sun beat down on their heads, and from the field a scent of warm grass and earth rose to their nostrils. Once, off in the distance, Barney heard a killdeer calling its name. He still remembered his father teaching him to recognize that birdsong.

Dick sat hunched up with his heels on the edge of the wall, nibbling on one stalk of timothy after another. When Barney came to the end of his story about the UFO, Dick straightened up and exclaimed, "Man! You're lucky!" He hit his knee with his fist. "I've always wanted to see a UFO. I wish I'd been here!"

Barney drew a deep breath. "I didn't know if you'd believe me."

Dick gave him another of his direct looks. "You're not the type to be making it up."

Barney stood up and walked away, fighting the strong emotion that surged through him. Dick believed him. He wasn't alone any more with this exciting, sometimes frightening, experience.

In a moment he had his feelings under control. He returned to the wall and boosted himself onto it.

"There's more," he said.

"More?" cried Dick. "You mean you saw the UFO again?"

"No. But I heard from the boy who was running it. His name's Tibbo."

Dick slid to the ground and began to pace back and forth as if he were too excited to sit still. "What does he look like?"

"I didn't see him. He was just a voice and a bunch of prickles."

"How's that?" Dick returned to his seat on the wall.

"The first night he came down in the silver ball, but I

didn't even know he was in it. After that, he stayed in the big space ship, several thousand miles up. But in a way he was down here with me." Barney frowned. He did not find it easy to explain Tibbo. He went on. "He talked to me and—and he sailed around like a flying porcupine without any body."

"This is too much!" exclaimed Dick.

Barney stared at him. "You don't want to hear any more?"

"Of course I do. I mean it's too much for me to understand all at once. It's great. Keep talking."

While Barney told about Tibbo's visits, Dick listened as if he had become part of the wall where he sat. He didn't move until Barney told how Tibbo had knocked down the barn. Then he turned around and gazed in awe at the heap of boards surrounding the framework.

Dick glanced at his watch. "I want to go up and look at what's left of the barn, but I can't do it now. I have to be home in fifteen minutes. Let's head back while we talk."

By the time Barney finished telling about his experiences with Tibbo, they had reached the road.

Dick sighed. "So you're going to Ornam. That'll be some excursion." He picked up his bike. "I wonder if Tibbo would take an extra passenger."

"I wish he would, but he can only take orphans," Barney reminded him.

"Oh, yeah. I forgot. Anyway, I'm not sure I want to be away that long, even on a trip to Ornam." He looked at Barney. "Do you know how long it would take to get there, even at the speed of light?"

Barney shook his head.

"I'd say at least five years. Tibbo told you his planet is in the Milky Way. The nearest Milky Way star system is Alpha Centauri. That's a group of three stars more than four light years from here. Ornam must be farther than that. Could be a lot farther."

Barney stared at him, stunned. "It'll be ten years before I can possibly get back to Earth. By then I'll be a man!"

What had he gotten himself into?

13 ⚡⚡⚡ A STRANGE MAGNETIC POWER

The next morning Dick arrived at nine-thirty.

"Let's go up and see what's left of the old barn," he suggested.

The day was warm and sunny and already most of the dew had left the grass as the boys started across the meadow.

"Did you tell your parents about the UFO and Tibbo?" asked Barney.

Dick looked surprised. "Of course not. I didn't think you'd want me to tell anyone."

"You're right. But I didn't ask you not to." Barney was pleased. Just as he had guessed, Dick was a person he could trust with a secret.

"Sometimes I wonder," Barney went on, "if I should let the Crandalls in on it now. You know, I didn't want to talk about the UFO before because then I thought I had a chance of being adopted, and I didn't want to do anything to rock the boat."

"But now that you're going to Ornam, it's different, too," said Dick.

Barney thought for a minute. "But if I tell them, they'll think they have to do something to keep me from going, even if they don't want to adopt me. Besides, if Scott gets wind of it, he'll—" Barney stopped, unable to talk for the lump in his throat. Leaving Scott was the worst part.

Dick's silence was answer enough. Barney knew no one could decide this problem for him.

Around the framework of the barn, boards and shingles were spread out over a large piece of ground. The boys walked all the way around it, picking up a board here and there.

"Let's make a pile of boards," said Barney. "Then Mrs. Crandall can look at them without climbing all over."

Soon they had a neat stack of silver-gray lumber.

"Do you notice something funny about these boards?" asked Dick. "Look, we haven't found a nail in any of them."

"And they aren't broken, either." Barney went back to the scattered wood that had covered the frame of the barn. "I see plenty of nails, but they're all loose. You know, on the ground or just lying on some of the planks."

"Very strange," commented Dick. "It gives me an

idea of the kind of power it took to knock this barn down.''

''It does? It doesn't tell me anything.''

''Here's the way I see it,'' said Dick. ''If all the nails came out of the barn, what would happen?''

''I suppose it would come apart. But how could they all come out at once? That barn went down fast.''

''I don't know exactly how it was done.'' Dick put his hands into his dungaree pockets and stared at the wrecked barn. ''But it seems to me that some kind of magnetic force circled the barn and pulled out all the nails at one clip.''

''Oh, man!'' said Barney in amazed wonder.

''Look here.'' Dick pointed to the boards that lay like fingers thrusting out from the sides of the wreckage. ''These must have flown away from the barn when it fell because they're on the outer edge. I think they came from the roof.''

''They did!'' Barney remembered. ''I saw the roof boards slide off. They sort of flew into the air.''

''Just what I thought.'' Dick nodded his head. He had a pleased expression in his eyes. He walked across the roof boards to the planks that lay close to the skeleton barn. ''These must be from the sides. I guess they dropped down and then toppled onto the grass. Look at the width of those boards. That one there must be two feet wide!''

''Mrs. Crandall will like that,'' said Barney. He bent

104

over and picked up a shingle. It was wooden and thicker at one end than at the other. "When the barn went down these were flying all over. At first I thought they were bats."

"It all ties in," said Dick. "That's just the way it would happen if the nails were all drawn out at once. By the way, those are handmade shingles."

"But the framework," objected Barney. "Why didn't that come down, too?"

Dick wore a wise grin. "That's more evidence in favor of my magnetic idea. In the old days they didn't use nails in the framework. They fastened the timbers together with wooden pegs."

"How do you know about all this?" asked Barney.

"Oh, we had a project on old tools when I was in fifth grade, and I got interested in how people used to build things in the early days. I read everything I could find and then Dad took me out to see some old barns."

"You ought to tell Mrs. Redding how you work at things you're interested in."

Dick shrugged. "What does it matter? I just study things because I want to know about them." He picked up several of the nails that were lying loose on the boards. "Take a look at these. Did you ever see any nails like this?"

Barney examined one of them. It didn't have much of a head on it, and instead of being round, it was almost square. "Nope. It's weird looking, all right."

"That's hand cut. Somebody cut that out of a flat piece of sheet iron with a hammer and chisel. It was a lot of work. And a strange thing about these nails, they're as straight as if they were new."

Dick slid the nails into his pocket and climbed back over the roof boards. "You know how a magnet picks up a nail? That's the kind of force Tibbo must have used on a large scale. I wish I had been here to see it happen. Barney, you have some very powerful friends."

The boys carried one of the wide boards back to the house. They laid it in the rear yard, and Barney hurried in to get Mrs. Crandall to come out and look at it.

She ran out, dressed in jeans and a faded blue shirt. Slowly she walked all around the board, bent and rubbed her hand lightly over it, turned it over, and then stood it up as if to see how it would look as wall paneling. Then she laid it carefully back onto the grass. All this time she did not say a word, but her face, shaded by the wings of her glossy black hair, shone with interest.

"Nice wood, isn't it?" remarked Dick.

Mrs. Crandall looked up at him from where she knelt on the grass. "It's the most beautiful board I have ever seen. It—it's almost alive. It has seen a lot, this old board, and it has held up well through all kinds of weather." She turned to Barney. "Are there more like this?"

"Lots more."

"Alex and I want to build on a family room," she

explained to Dick. "We want a place where Barney and Scott can have their friends in to play and talk and sit around the fire and toast marshmallows. Things like that. And we'll dance there, Alex's friends and mine, and we can teach you and Barney, and Kara, too, all kinds of dances, if you're interested." She asked Barney, "How does that sound to you?"

"Great!" Barney tried to act enthusiastic. It did sound great, he thought. Only he probably wouldn't be here to see it. He wouldn't even be here to gather up the wood from the barn. Tibbo had said they'd be leaving in a few days.

Dick took the square nails from his pocket and put them into Mrs. Crandall's hand. "Thought you might be interested in these."

"You're right!" she exclaimed. "Do you suppose there are enough good ones like this so we can use them to fasten up a few of the boards in the new family room?"

Barney cut in. "There are enough to do the whole room!"

Mrs. Crandall seemed amazed. "I thought they'd be all bent and twisted."

Barney said no more. It could be hard to explain those straight nails if she began to ask questions.

"I'd better go home now," said Dick. He went after his bike that he had left leaning against the garage.

Barney walked up the driveway with him. "You

going to practice this afternoon?" he asked.

"Sure. How about we meet at the school bus stop at about two-fifteen?"

"Okay."

Dick paused at the end of the driveway. "Barney, I don't understand why you're so sure the Crandalls don't want you."

"I already explained what Rabbit told me and what I heard Mr. Crandall say."

"I don't know about that," said Dick. "But the way Mrs. Crandall talked about that family room, she sounds as if she's counting on having you and Scott grow up here."

"I noticed that," said Barney. "Maybe she wants me, but Mr. Crandall doesn't."

After Dick left, Barney kept thinking about what his friend had said. He wished he could believe he was wanted, but he couldn't, not after what he had heard with his own ears. The only reason he was still here was because the Crandalls were kind people and they didn't want to hurt him.

Even if they kept him, Barney didn't want to be adopted because of pity.

14   SEASON!

As Barney and Dick left the bus stop on their bikes that afternoon, a blue car whizzed by, honking at them.

That reminded Barney of his experience with Mr. Jardine, so he told Dick about it.

"I wish I'd gone back to talk with him right then," he said. "Now I hate the thought of meeting him again."

"Well, you could still talk with him if you'd feel any better," suggested Dick. "I can't see that you did anything terrible, anyway. I know Mr. Jardine. He blows up at nothing, but he gets over it fast."

Barney shook his head. "I don't see how I could face him."

The ball practice went well that afternoon. Barney still didn't have a glove of his own, but Jake had brought along an old one for him to use.

Mr. MacDougall began at once to find out the strong and weak points of the players. Soon he had the team reorganized.

Barney was pleased when he was put in as catcher. He was so wrapped up in the practice, it was not until they broke up at five o'clock that he noticed how the line of interested spectators had grown.

He and Dick walked toward their bikes.

"There he is," said Dick.

"Who?"

"Mr. Jardine. Your pal who almost ran into you."

Barney stole a quick glance toward the people who had been watching the practice. Yes, that did look like the man who had shouted for him to come back and talk, only now that he was not red faced and angry he didn't seem like the same person.

"Here's your chance," said Dick.

"*Uh*—you mean talk to him—now?"

"You'll never have a better set-up. I'm beginning to know you, Barney. You worry about things like that. You might as well get it over."

Dick was right. Barney's knees felt wobbly, but the man was looking his way now and his expression gave Barney courage. Swallowing hard, Barney said, "Here goes."

He broke away from Dick and walked across the gravel. The man had stopped and seemed to be waiting for him.

"Don't I know you?" he asked Barney. "You look familiar but I can't place you."

"I'm Barney Galloway. I was riding my bike the other day and—" He couldn't think what to say next.

"Oh, yes." Mr. Jardine looked him up and down. "You're the kid who shot in front of me. Gave me the scare of my life. You could've caused a bad accident."

"Y-yes, sir." Barney was shaking, but he decided to explain what had happened. "I was thinking of something else so I didn't notice that other car pulling out."

"So you think both of us ought to get after that other driver," remarked Mr. Jardine.

"Well, no. I ought to look ahead more."

"You should, at that. I could've hit you," said Mr. Jardine. "We're lucky no one was hurt. In fact, we were lucky all the way. I didn't even dent the lamppost or bend my bumper." He seemed to be tired of the subject. "So let's forget it." He held out his hand and Barney put his into it. "We'll both be more careful from now on. Glad to have met you, Barney."

Barney's face was still red when he rejoined Dick.

"How'd it go?" asked Dick.

"All right. He was really great, considering the trouble I caused him."

As the boys rode down the street, they passed Mr. Jardine who was on foot. He waved a friendly hand and Barney waved back. He did feel better.

Dinner was almost ready when he reached home, but he had time to tell Mr. Crandall about the softball prac-

111

tice and his new position as catcher.

"You'll need a catcher's mitt." Mr. Crandall folded the newspaper he had been reading and laid it on the coffee table. "You plan to be here when I get home from work tomorrow and we'll go to town and buy one."

Barney hesitated. That surely didn't sound as if Mr. Crandall didn't want to keep him. Barney didn't know what to think, except that he didn't want Mr. Crandall to buy him a mitt that he might never have a chance to use. "Probably I can get one from the kid who used to be catcher. He's playing shortstop now."

Mr. Crandall smiled his approval. "That's a good idea. See what the fellow wants for his glove, and make sure it fits."

All during the month and a half he had stayed in the house near Pineville, Barney had been too shy and afraid of saying the wrong thing to carry on much of a conversation with Mr. Crandall, but now he found him easy to talk to. He told him all about his second meeting with Mr. Jardine.

Mr. Crandall's sandy brows arched in surprise. "I have to hand it to you. That took courage."

As they walked into the dining room for dinner, he put his arm across Barney's shoulders. He said quietly, "I'm proud of you, Son."

Son! The word seemed to stab through Barney's

112

chest. Mr. Crandall sounded as if he meant it! Was it possible Dick was right and his foster parents really wanted him? Barney felt hope warm him as if he had stepped into the sunshine.

Scott came out of the kitchen carefully carrying a basket of rolls which he set on the table. "I'm helping," he announced.

"Nice going, Tiger," said Barney. He spoke automatically, for his mind was busy, wondering. Had he found just what he wanted, a home for both of them, and then thrown it away?

After dinner he rode his bicycle to Dick's. He had to talk to his friend.

He had never been to the Williams' home, but Dick had told him how to get there. It was on the same street as the school bus stop, only half a block to the left.

The Williams' place turned out to be a pleasant white ranch house with black shutters.

Dick came out when Barney turned into the driveway, and after introducing him to his parents, took him to his room.

"I'd know this was your pad," commented Barney. There were shelves with books on all subjects, but especially on astronomy and space travel. On the top shelf was a small model of the solar system with planets on wires grouped around the sun. The room was neater than Barney's, which was no surprise, either.

As usual, Barney came right to the point. "I don't think I want to go to Ornam."

"I don't blame you," said Dick. "Well, tell Tibbo you've changed your mind."

"Yeah, but I promised him."

"I believe you have grounds for canceling your reservation," said Dick. "I don't think Tibbo played fair with you. He didn't tell you it would take at least five years to get to Ornam, for instance."

"N-no."

Dick went on like a lawyer stating a case. "It's what's called misrepresentation. You were conned into taking a trip when you didn't know what it entailed."

"Okay, I believe you. But how can I back out if Tibbo doesn't come again? Maybe he'll wait until it's time to leave for Ornam and then come and scoop me up whether I want to go or not."

Dick prowled restlessly around the room, straightening pictures that were already straight. "Yeah. You have a point there."

"And it's more than just me," Barney went on. "What about those people the Garks rescue from drowning and things like that? They don't have a chance. They get shanghaied to Ornam."

"Of course, if it weren't for the Garks, they'd be dead," Dick pointed out.

"I know that. But shouldn't they still have a choice?

Besides, if our government or the government of other countries knew the Garks wanted people to visit their planet, there might be lots of people who'd like to go."

Dick stopped pacing and dropped into a chair. "Man, you've come up with some tough questions and I don't know the answers."

"That's the trouble," said Barney. "Neither do I. I think we ought to talk to someone. Maybe the President."

"Of the U.S.A.?"

"Yeah. If he knew the Garks were here, I bet he'd arrange to give them a big welcome and take them on a tour of the country."

"Somehow I don't think he'd believe us. We'd better start with someone we know. How about the Crandalls?"

"I don't want to get them all stirred up."

Dick leaned forward with his hands on his bony knees. "They might not believe you, anyway. My parents wouldn't. They don't believe in UFO's *at all*. We ought to talk to someone who knows something about space travel. Someone who believes in UFO's." He snapped to alert. "I've got it! Mr. Wexel."

"Our science teacher? Could be."

Dick said excitedly, "I was talking with him one day after school, and he said there must be life on other planets and that someday the people, or whatever they are, would try to get in touch with us.''

"Sounds good," admitted Barney.

"Want to go see him?"

"I guess so."

"All right," said Dick. "He lives in Valmora. I'll call him and see if he can talk to us tomorrow."

"Kind of a hard bike ride," Barney objected. "Especially that hill just before you get to town."

"There's a bus." Dick was ready to solve all problems. "It picks up passengers at the school bus stop. I'll find out the schedule and give you a call. You can ride up here and leave your bike."

"I get an allowance and I haven't spent much of it," said Barney. "I'm sure the Crandalls won't mind if I take a trip to Valmora."

15 ⚡⚡⚡ RUNAWAY TRUCK

At nine-thirty the next morning Barney and Dick caught the bus for Valmora.

The bus was almost full, but they found room to sit in the center of the back seat that extended the full width of the vehicle.

The route took them east through Pineville and then into open, hilly country. From his position in the center of the rear seat, Barney could see down the aisle and through the front windshield.

Within a few minutes they started to climb up the steep hill outside Valmora. When they reached the top, the little town, slightly larger than Pineville, lay below them in the valley. It was a pretty sight with its white houses and green lawns and three church spires reaching above all the other buildings.

Barney noticed that traffic was tied up about two-thirds of the way down the hill. When they drew nearer he could see the problem. A huge tractor-trailer was lying on its side across the eastbound lane. Traffic was blocked in both directions. Police cars and tow trucks with flashing lights were already on the scene.

Dick leaned back in his seat and closed his eyes. "Wake me up when we come to our stop."

Barney was not surprised. He knew how Dick hated to wait, especially when he didn't have a book to read.

The bus reached the end of the line of cars and came to a complete standstill.

Soon the police opened westbound traffic, and cars began coming up the hill. The road downhill was still solidly blocked.

Suddenly Barney felt his skin tingle. Tibbo was watching again!

"Tibbo's here," Barney whispered.

Dick opened one eye and said, "Good. Maybe you'll get a chance to talk to him." Then he slumped down in the seat again.

A loud, continuous horn blast sounded behind the bus. Barney turned around to look out the rear window. To his horror, he saw a huge gravel truck roaring down the hill. The driver was leaning on the horn as the truck rushed toward them, swaying from side to side, narrowly missing the oncoming cars and spraying them and the road with gravel from the full load.

Barney shouted, "Runaway truck!" and dived for the floor, pulling Dick with him. The other people in the rear seat leaped past them.

At once the aisle was clogged with passengers trying

to get out the front and side doors. But already the scream of the horn was deafening. Only two or three people had time to escape.

Barney braced for the crash.

But instead of the crunch of metal hitting metal, there was silence. Even the horn had stopped blowing, and the frightened cries of the passengers were stilled.

For a moment Barney lay unbelieving on the floor of the bus. Then he scrambled to his feet and looked toward the rear window. The nose of the truck was only inches away. It had stopped just in time.

Dick sat up and stared at the gravel truck. "Thanks for dragging me to the floor, pal."

Barney thought he was complaining. "You'd have been glad I did if that truck had hit."

"Doggonit, Barney! I'm serious. I could've been tossed through a window."

All the people in the bus were talking excitedly and trying to get out of the two doors. Since they had been in the rear, Barney and Dick were almost the last to leave.

When they got outside, the truck driver was standing on the road beside the cab, his face red and perspiring.

"I don't *know* what happened!" he was shouting. "My brakes gave out and I couldn't get into low gear. Then all at once it just stopped—like—like someone dropped a mattress or a cushion of air in front of me."

The bus driver was pale. "Thank heavens you man-

119

aged to stop. What a crackup that would've been!''

The trucker repeated, ''I don't know how I stopped! The brakes didn't take hold. My truck's only standing still now because I managed to get it in parking gear after I stopped.''

Barney and Dick looked at each other.

''Tibbo?'' asked Dick in a low voice.

Barney nodded. ''It must have been Tibbo. What else could have kept that truck from crashing into the bus?''

The boys walked away from the crowd.

''You said 'Tibbo's here' a couple of minutes before the truck came down the hill,'' recalled Dick. ''Is he still watching now?''

''No, the prickles have gone. But I felt them when we were lying on the floor,'' said Barney. ''He saved our lives. He saved everyone on the bus and the truck driver, too.''

''Did you ask him to help?''

''No. It all happened so fast I didn't have time to think.''

Dick pushed back a lock of hair with a hand that shook slightly. ''You know why he stopped the truck, don't you?''

''I suppose so.'' Barney met Dick's eyes. ''He's not going to let me get killed. He wants to take me to Ornam.'' He felt weighted down. ''How can I back out of the trip now?'' he asked. ''I owe Tibbo my life.''

16 ✄✄✄ INVISIBLE SPACE SHIP

Barney and Dick were half an hour late for their appointment with Mr. Wexel, but he didn't seem to mind.

The teacher took them to his comfortable screened porch and poured glasses of cold ginger ale.

Then he sat down in a wicker chair with his knees crossed. "Now let's have it. You must have something important on your mind to bring you all the way here."

"It's important," said Dick. "It may affect the whole world."

Mr. Wexel looked surprised, but he only nodded and motioned for Dick to continue.

Taking turns and interrupting each other, the boys gave the science teacher all of the details of Barney's experience with the visitor from outer space, beginning with the prickly feeling of his skin and the sensation of being watched. They brought their account up to date by telling about the close call on the Valmora hill.

Every now and then Mr. Wexel broke in to ask a

question. Barney could see that he was deeply interested.

When they had finished, the man was silent for a moment. Then he said, "As I understand it, Barney, you're the only one who saw the UFO and you're the only one who has heard Tibbo."

"As far as I know, I am," answered Barney.

"Have you talked to your foster parents about this?"

"No," said Barney. "You're the only one I've told except for Dick."

"So the Crandalls didn't see the UFO and they haven't heard Tibbo?"

"That's right," said Barney. He could guess what Mr. Wexel was thinking.

Dick backed up his friend. "I saw the barn that Tibbo knocked down, and it was no windstorm that took that apart. It had to be an unusual force that would pull out all the nails."

"True, true," said the teacher. "Still, if it were anyone but you two I'd say you were pulling my leg."

Barney's hopes rose slightly. Perhaps Mr. Wexel did believe them. He saw by Dick's face that he, too, was encouraged.

"I'd stake my reputation on your honesty and common sense. So the only answer I can come up with is that someone is playing a very clever trick on Barney."

Barney leaned back in his chair, feeling as if he had

been punched in the stomach. Neither he nor Dick said a word. The teacher's idea was logical, Barney had to admit. He had had the same thought himself after Tibbo's first visit.

Mr. Wexel went on, as if he were thinking out loud. "Your room may be wired, Barney, so someone can transmit to you. But that isn't the whole story because this—visitor—"

"Tibbo," prompted Barney.

"Yes, Tibbo. He talked to you outdoors in the meadow."

Dick broke in. "What about the truck? Tibbo stopped that just inches from the bus."

Mr. Wexel waved his hand as if brushing aside a troublesome fly. "You don't *know* that Tibbo had anything to do with the truck. It's more likely that the brakes took hold at the last minute."

"The prickling in the air," said Dick. "How do you explain that?"

"That could be imagination."

"And the UFO—the space ship. You said someday we'd be contacted by life from outer space," Dick reminded him. "Now it has happened."

"Dick, there are some holes in this story. I'm sure someone would have noticed the silver ball Barney described."

"Tibbo told me the Garks know how to fool radar

and telescopes," said Barney. "Maybe they can make their space ships invisible when they want to."

"Perhaps." Mr. Wexel did not sound convinced. "What about the big space ship? How far up did you say it is?"

"Several thousand miles."

"*Hm,* of course it would have to be high," mused Mr. Wexel. "Still, radar could pick it up. Besides, there's an observatory at Valmora College, and I have several friends who are astronomers. They keep an eye out for anything new in the sky."

"But a little thing like a space ship up that high—" began Barney.

Mr. Wexel lifted a silencing hand. "You're right, it wouldn't be visible by day, but it would show up just after sunset when the sky is getting dark. The sun's rays would hit the ship and make it shine. It would look like a small star. You might even see it with the naked eye."

"What if some astronomer saw it and thought it was a Russian satellite?" asked Dick.

"Could be, but he'd have mentioned it. Besides, you said there are other ships posted all around the Earth. Some of them would have been reported by now."

Dick finished his ginger ale and set down the empty glass. "Thanks for listening, Mr. Wexel. We'd better be going."

"Wait a minute," said the teacher. "We have to examine all the angles. Suppose the space ships *are* hovering over the Earth and somehow they haven't been seen. It could be a dangerous situation. Some foreign power in our own world may be behind this."

"I suppose so." Dick sounded skeptical.

Barney was sure Tibbo had not come from a country on Earth. Neither had the space ship. However, he said nothing. They had told Mr. Wexel everything that had happened. If he didn't believe now, there was no use trying to persuade him.

Mr. Wexel went on. "I'll call the observatory at the college. I'll talk with my friends in the Air Force, too, and have them make a thorough search."

"Thank you!" said Barney. He felt better. At least Mr. Wexel was going to help, whether he believed them or not. The astronomers would surely find the Garks' space ships and someone would tell the President. Barney felt that the responsibility had been shifted from his shoulders. It was a great relief.

The science teacher got to his feet. "Come on. I'll give you a ride back to Dick's house. I have to go to Pineville, anyway." He put his hand on Barney's shoulder. "I'll give you a call in a few days after I do some investigating. But if I were you I wouldn't pack my bag for that trip to Ornam. Get outdoors and have a good time and forget all of this business about visitors from outer space."

He doesn't believe me, that's sure, thought Barney. But when he checks with the astronomers and the Air Force he'll change his mind.

By the time Barney reached home, lunch was over and Scott was having a nap. While eating his lunch in the kitchen, he watched Mrs. Crandall hull strawberries for the shortcake they were going to have for dessert that night.

After lunch he went up to his room. There he wandered around trying to decide what to do. He opened a book, but he couldn't keep his mind on the words. Then he went to his desk and started a letter to his friend Howie in Buffalo. He got as far as the date and "Dear Howie." Finally he wrote: "The other night I woke up and climbed out on the roof and saw a UFO. It looked like a silver ball with a ring around it."

Barney tossed down his pen and discarded the letter in the wastebasket. How could anyone believe that? Howie would think he had taken up writing science fiction.

The phone rang and he could hear Mrs. Crandall answering it. A moment later he heard her calling softly so as not to awaken Scott.

"Barney, it's for you."

He ran lightly down the stairs. Maybe it was Mr. Wexel. He had said it would be a few days, but perhaps he had gotten in touch with the observatory right away.

126

Barney picked up the phone. It was Dick. "Do you feel like sitting around and waiting to hear from Mr. Wexel?"

"I'm going bananas already."

"Same here," said Dick. "I have an idea. My uncle has a farm on Lake Tomega. It's only about ten miles from here. How'd you like to go over there and camp out in the meadow behind his woods for two or three days? It's right on the lake and we could go fishing and swimming."

"Man!" breathed Barney.

Dick chuckled. "I thought you'd go along with the idea. Find out what the Crandalls say and let me know. I have a tent big enough for the two of us and a couple of sleeping bags. We can start early tomorrow morning on our bikes."

17 ⚡⚡⚡ TIBBO IS STUBBORN

The campfire, fed with driftwood, still burned long after Dick and Barney had cooked their dinner over it.

They sat behind the fire, gazing out over the lake.

"This was the best day of my whole life," said Barney.

"Mine, too," agreed Dick.

Barney leaned against a rock and dug his bare toes into the sand that was still warmed by the sun although it was past seven o'clock. He was contented and full of hot dogs, baked beans, marshmallows, and the apple pie that Dick's aunt had brought out to them.

If Tibbo came for him tomorrow, at least he'd had this perfect day. Even the bicycle trip here had been fun, although it was hard work going up some of the hills. Catching a fish and eating it for lunch, swimming with Dick's aunt and uncle in Lake Tomego, building the campfire, all had added up to make this a day to remember.

128

Behind him the two-man tent was standing with the sleeping bags ready.

"This is the first time I ever went camping," Barney said. "I'm glad you thought of it."

"How about a game of checkers?" suggested Dick. "I brought along my pocket set."

"All right, but I'm not much good at it. You're probably a champ."

"Yeah. You guessed it," said Dick, putting on a modest expression.

He opened the tiny checkerboard on the flat rock they had used for a picnic table.

"Red or black?" he asked.

"Red."

In a few minutes Dick had won two games.

"Oh, come on, Barney. Put your mind on it. This isn't even fun."

"I *am* doing the best I can."

"Plan your moves."

"I'll try. But every time I figure out some smart play you make a move that spoils it." Barney set up the checkers again, and the game started. Again Dick was winning.

Halfway through Barney looked up. "Tibbo's watching. Maybe he's here. The prickles are strong."

"Well, find out," said Dick.

A cheerful voice sounded in Barney's ears. "How

come you didn't invite me on this camping trip?''

"How could I?'' asked Barney. ''You didn't come to see me.''

"What are you talking about?'' inquired Dick.

"Can't you hear Tibbo? He's right beside me.''

"No. You're the only one I heard.'' Dick sounded cross. ''Tell him to talk so I can hear him, too.''

"No way.'' Tibbo answered for himself. ''I'm in enough trouble for talking to you.''

Barney passed the word to Dick. ''He won't do it. The Garks wouldn't like it.''

"Oh. Can he hear me?''

"Of course I can hear him,'' said Tibbo. ''What's that game you're playing?''

"Checkers,'' answered Barney. To Dick he said, ''He can hear you, and he wants to know what we're playing.''

"Hi, Tibbo,'' said Dick. ''Welcome to the party.''

"That's very nice of him, especially since he can't hear me,'' remarked Tibbo. ''Start playing again so I can get the hang of it.''

Dick and Barney finished the game.

"Barney, you're a lousy player,'' said Tibbo. ''You had him cornered twice and you let him get away.''

"If you know so much about it, why don't you play next time?''

"I will.'' Tibbo sounded pleased. ''Set up the check-

130

ers. I'll tell you how to move.''

"He wants to play," Barney explained.

"Okay. Ready." Dick was wearing a grin. "This is no doubt the first interplanetary checker contest in history. Since you're our guest, you start first, Tibbo."

All through the game Tibbo told Barney which checker to move. He was a fast, clever player, and as he directed his plays, Barney began to understand some of the strategy.

Dick wasn't happy as Barney scooped the black checkers from the board. "It's not fair, Tibbo. I'll bet you're using a computer to figure out your moves."

Barney laughed. "He says he's just using his brain, and it's about ten thousand years ahead of yours."

Tibbo won the next four games.

"I know how you feel now," Dick said to Barney.

"Tibbo says you're fairly smart for an Earth boy." Barney couldn't stop laughing.

Dick folded up the checker set. "Now's your chance to tell him you don't want to go to Ornam."

"What's that?" demanded Tibbo.

"I hate to tell you," said Barney. "But I'd rather not go to Ornam. I didn't know it would take five years to get there and another five to get back. That's too long."

"What's ten years?" asked Tibbo.

"In ten years I'll be in my twenties. I'll miss an awful lot."

131

"You won't get old as fast when you're traveling close to the speed of light."

"Why not?"

"Just because you won't. It's a scientific fact that space travelers who go that fast don't age as much."

"What did he say?" asked Dick.

Barney repeated the conversation and added, "I suppose if I came back in ten years Scott and I would be about the same age. He'd keep on getting older at the same rate as usual, but I wouldn't."

"That's about right," came Tibbo's voice. "Only you won't be coming back in ten years. Our plan is to return in one hundred years."

"One hundred years!" cried Barney. This was far worse than he had feared. "By then everyone I know will be dead. Even Scott."

"On Ornam we live to be one thousand," said Tibbo proudly. "If you decide to stay there you'll also live to be a thousand."

"No, Tibbo," said Barney firmly. "I'm not going. I don't think the Crandalls would want me to go, either."

Tibbo's voice was stubborn. "The plans are made."

"I mean it," insisted Barney. "Don't come after me."

Silence was his only answer.

"Tibbo!"

Still no answer.

Barney tried pleading. "I know I shouldn't back out after I said I'd go. But you weren't fair. A hundred years! That's more than most lifetimes on Earth."

Tibbo said nothing.

"He won't talk about it," Barney told Dick. "I'd think he was gone, but I still feel the prickles."

Finally Dick said, "Ask him where the space ship is."

Tibbo's voice came from the other side of the campfire, as jaunty as ever. "Don't you wish you knew?"

When Barney and Dick had put out the fire and were ready to crawl into their sleeping bags, Tibbo said, "Don't go to sleep yet. I'll be lonesome."

"Why don't you join us?" Barney invited.

"May I?"

Barney put the question to Dick. "Tibbo's lonesome," he explained.

"All right," agreed Dick. "But I think he ought to promise not to take you to Ornam."

"That's none of his business," declared Tibbo in an annoyed tone.

Barney slid into his sleeping bag.

Dick was on his knees, ready to pull up the zipper on the tent flap. "Is he inside?"

"Yes," said Barney. "But you don't have to worry about Tibbo. A little thing like a closed tent flap wouldn't keep him out. He can go through walls or anything." He reached for his jacket and spread it on the floor of the tent beside him. "You can sleep here, Tibbo. Is that all right?"

"Thanks, Barney. I don't really need any place special."

Silence enclosed the tent. Barney could hear the lapping sound of waves touching the shore and the chirp of crickets in the meadow behind their camping place. He was ready to go to sleep but the prickly feeling of electricity in the air kept him awake.

Finally he asked quietly, "Tibbo, can you turn off those prickles? I can't get to sleep."

"I'll try."

In a minute the space boy's voice asked, "That better?"

"I can feel them a little, but not enough to bother me. Thanks. Good night, Tibbo."

"Good night, Barney. Good night, Dick."

Dick stirred. In a drowsy voice he said, "Good night, Tibbo." He sat up straight, his brown hair on end. "Barney, did you say, 'Good night, Dick'?"

"No. But Tibbo did."

"I heard him! I think I did. I was asleep." Dick lay down again and repeated, "Good night, Tibbo."

Barney heard Tibbo laugh.

When Barney awakened the next morning, Tibbo was gone.

134

During breakfast Dick suddenly burst out, "Doggonit, Barney, you can't take off with Tibbo! I don't want you to leave. We have too much fun together."

"I don't want to go." The bread Barney had browned over the campfire and spread with jam had tasted delicious a moment ago. Now it seemed dry and it stuck in his throat. With an effort he swallowed it. "What can I do? Tibbo said, 'The plans are made.' After that he wouldn't even talk about it."

"Just don't go. If he comes for you, refuse to leave the house."

"You know what he did to the barn. He could do the same thing to the house and pick me out of it like one of the nails. Dick, there's no use trying to fight the Garks. They're too far ahead of us in science."

"Try, though," begged Dick.

"I will. My best hope's Mr. Wexel. When he finds out there really is a space ship up there, maybe he and his astronomer friends can figure some way of getting in touch with it."

Barney took a drink of his lukewarm cocoa before he went on. "Now I don't see why I ever told Tibbo I'd go. I was really down that night. I had had that tangle with Mr. Jardine, and I was sure the Crandalls didn't want me."

"I think you worry too much," said Dick. "And

135

there's another thing. How come you act so stiff around the Crandalls? I'd almost think you didn't like them. If you always treat them like that, it's no wonder Mr. Crandall wants to send you back."

"What do you mean? Look, ever since I've gone there I've walked the line. I've done everything I could to help."

"Yeah. And you still call them Mr. and Mrs. Crandall. Scott has more sense than you do. At least he says Mom and Dad. Don't you know that's what they want?"

"Oh." Barney considered this. "It's hard to call them that when they're not my real parents."

"I suppose it is," said Dick. "But if I couldn't have my own parents, I'd pick the Crandalls."

For the rest of the boys' campout there was no sign of Tibbo. Barney and Dick spent most of the time in the water or on it in a boat. During one night it rained, but they slept warm and dry in the little tent.

The third day they broke camp and headed home. The ride seemed shorter than before. Yet Barney was tired when he wheeled into the driveway at five o'clock.

The house looked like home to him. He had a warm, happy feeling at the thought of seeing Scott and Finn and the Crandalls and his own room again.

As soon as the door opened, Finn burst out like a tornado. He leaped all over his master and covered his face with wet kisses.

Mrs. Crandall hugged Barney. "Nice to have you home." She sniffed. "You smell like a campfire."

"Hi, Barney!" Mr. Crandall took his duffel bag and gave him a friendly pat on the back.

They went into the house where Barney caught the scent of chicken cooking. The sound of music came from the kitchen. He wondered if Mrs. Crandall, Mom—he tried the name out in his mind—had been dancing.

"Where's Scott?" he asked.

"He's over at Kara's," said Mrs. Crandall. "Alex got home early this afternoon so we decided to go up to the old barn and get some of the wood. We were afraid Scott might get hurt climbing around on the boards, so we took him to MacDougalls'. He's invited to stay for dinner. Oh, Barney, those planks are beautiful! But we still can't figure out why the barn fell down in such a strange way."

Mr. Crandall set the duffel at the foot of the stairs. "You had a phone call from Mr. Wexel a few minutes ago. He said to tell you no one could find a UFO. What's that all about?"

18 ⚡⚡⚡ A STRANGE STORY

Barney stood in the dim light of the hallway, one hand on Finn's head, trying to digest this news.

No one could find a UFO. That meant Mr. Wexel's experts had failed to locate any of the space ships from Ornam. Tibbo was right. The Garks must have some way of making them invisible, and hiding them from radar, too.

Mr Crandall repeated, "What's this about a UFO?"

Barney followed him to the kitchen, his mind working rapidly. He could easily put aside the question by saying someone had reported a UFO and Mr. Wexel was going to try to find out if any astronomers or the Air Force had located one.

Mrs. Crandall was standing at the work shelf. Barney watched her shake up a bottle of salad dressing and pour it over a bowl of greens and tomatoes. He had never cared much for lettuce and stuff like that before he came here, but she made good salads.

Mr. Crandall was waiting. Barney looked up and met his penetrating blue eyes. He didn't want to lie to this man, and what was the use of keeping all of this to himself any longer? Soon he'd be on his way to Ornam, whether he wanted to go or not, and he'd like to have his foster parents know where he'd gone.

"I saw a UFO, a space ship," he said clearly. "One night last week. It came up close to the house. And the next night I had a visitor—a boy—from the planet Ornam. His name is Tibbo."

Mrs. Crandall dropped the spoon and fork with which she had been tossing the salad.

Mr. Crandall nervously raked his fingers through his sand-colored hair. His eyes had a puzzled expression as he studied Barney's face. "Is this a joke?" he asked.

"No. It's exactly what happened, and there's lots more."

"We want to hear it all," the man assured him. "Let's sit down." He crossed to the kitchen table where three places were set.

"It'll take a long time to tell," said Barney.

"Oh." Mr. Crandall looked around as if he had forgotten where he was. "Is dinner ready, hon?"

"All ready to serve. I thought we'd eat out here since there are just the three of us."

Mr. Crandall stood up. "Suppose you go wash, Barney, while Lois and I get the food on the table."

They let him tell his story at his own speed. Even Finn was ready to be still. He lay beside Barney's chair as if contented just to be near him.

"No hurry," Mr. Crandall encouraged. "We have all evening."

"And take time to eat," said Mrs. Crandall. "You must be starved after that long bike ride."

"I am." Barney hungrily bit into a chicken leg. After the edge was off his appetite he began to talk. The words flowed more and more easily as his listeners' interest drew him on. All through dinner he talked and ate and answered their questions.

When at last his plate was clean, he was surprised to see that his foster parents had eaten very little.

In his account, he had come to the night when he'd agreed to go to Ornam.

"Why did you want to go?" asked Mr. Crandall.

"*Uh*—it was sort of a way out."

"A way out of what?"

"I just told you what Rabbit said, that you wanted a little boy like Scott."

"Oh, and you thought we took you to get Scott?"

"Yes."

"We did."

Barney looked up at Mr. Crandall, surprised to hear him state this so honestly.

Mr. Crandall went on. "But that was before we got

140

acquainted with you. Now nothing would make us give you up.''

''We knew all along we wanted two children.'' Mrs. Crandall's dark eyes shone with the same honesty as her husband's. ''That first day when we brought you and Scott home and saw how fond you were of each other, we thought, 'How perfect! Now we have our family.' ''

''But how about you, Barney?'' asked Mr. Crandall. ''Sometimes we've wondered if you felt at home here. Would you rather live someplace else? Is that why you told Tibbo you'd go?''

Barney looked at the two people across from him. Dick was right. They were the best parents anyone could find, and he knew that he loved them. But still—one dark memory tormented him.

''The other night when I went down the hall to the bathroom,'' began Barney, his eyes on Mr. Crandall, ''I didn't mean to listen, but I heard you say, 'It's time to get rid of him.' So I figured I didn't have a chance.''

Mr. Crandall looked blank. ''I don't remember saying that.''

Barney's face felt hot, but he went on. ''Then Mrs. Crandall said, ''Have you no heart?''

His foster parents looked at each other. Suddenly Mrs. Crandall burst into laughter. Yet there were tears in her eyes. When she could speak, she said, ''George—old George, my car! You had so much trouble fixing it, and you said, "It's time to get rid of him.' "

Mr. Crandall reached over and hugged her. "I did! I remember."

Barney watched them, gradually realizing the truth. "So you weren't talking about me. You didn't want me to go."

Mr. Crandall was still smiling. "I never want you to go."

Barney didn't have to think about his answer. "Then I want to stay—Dad."

"I've waited a long time to hear you say that, Barney." Mr. Crandall's voice was hoarse.

They all got up from the table and went into the living room where Barney told them about Tibbo's visit while he and Dick were camping and how the space boy had shared their tent.

"You say Dick thought he heard Tibbo?" asked Mr. Crandall.

"Yes, just once. He wasn't sure."

"What does he think about all of this? Does he believe it?"

"Yes. He says I'm not the kind to make up things."

"And you're not," agreed Mr. Crandall. "But it's a strange story."

"You don't believe me?" Barney was shocked. They had seemed so understanding.

142

"I didn't say that. But what would you think if Lois or I told you a story like this?"

Barney considered. He even managed a smile. "I'd think you were bonkers."

"I don't think that. But there's a possibility you imagined some of this. You've been under a lot of pressure ever since you lost your parents. The way I see it, you've been like a father to Scott."

Mrs. Crandall added, "And all those TV programs on space—"

"If only a UFO had been sighted," mused the man. "Or if Dick were sure he heard Tibbo."

Barney searched his mind for proof of his experience. "What about the barn? And the way all the nails came out of the wood?"

"That's odd, all right," agreed Mr. Crandall.

"Handy for us, too," added his wife. "We don't have to pull out all those nails. Alex, I don't think it's important right now whether or not we believe in Tibbo. We believe in Barney, and when he tells us something we know he thinks it's true."

"Right. We're with you all the way, Son." He looked at the clock. "I'd better go after Scott. Want to come along?"

Barney jumped up. "Yes!" He chuckled and added, "Dad."

Mrs. Crandall came over and put her arms around

143

him. "You're ours, Barney. Tell Tibbo we won't let you go."

"I will. But I might have to go. The Garks are powerful."

"We're your legal guardians," said Mr. Crandall. "You can tell Tibbo no one has any right to take you without our permission."

Barney was confused. One minute he was sure his new parents didn't believe in Tibbo and the next they were talking as if they knew him personally.

Mrs. Crandall started toward the kitchen, then turned back. "Alex, I think it would be better not to mention any of this to Scott. If he hears that Barney might go away, he'll be broken hearted."

"I've been thinking the same thing, hon. We won't tell the MacDougalls, either. All right, Barney?"

Barney said jokingly, "If you don't tell anyone, how're we going to get on television?"

19 ⚑⚑⚑ THE SPACE SHIP RETURNS

Tired from his camping trip, Barney went to bed early Friday night. He slept soundly, and Tibbo did not come to visit or to spirit him away.

When he awakened it was still early, but already the sun lay like a warm gold patch on the rug beside his bed.

The scent of freshly brewed coffee came up the stairs from the kitchen.

Barney lay on his back and slowly pivoted his head from one side to the other, studying his room.

His room. He let himself dream that this comfortable room would be his until he grew up. Even if he went away to college or to work, he could still come back to it.

He turned on his side so he could look out the window at the slope of Mount Casper. This winter he and Scott and their new dad and mom could slide down the hill on the toboggan he had seen stored in the garage.

Dick had skis, and Barney was quite sure Mr. Cran— no, Dad—would buy him a pair.

And the Patriots. He could play ball with them all summer. Even without Tibbo's help, if he worked hard, he could be a good player.

Tibbo's name brought him back to reality. This daydream of happiness on Earth could come true only if he didn't have to go to Ornam.

The trip to a distant planet had lost its glamour. Now it seemed like an endless journey in a traveling prison. No wonder Tibbo spoke English like a native. He'd had five years to study it on the way and nothing much else to do. Besides, he was a fast learner. Look how quickly he had caught on to checkers!

That afternoon Barney met Dick at the school bus stop and they rode their bicycles to Pineville for softball practice.

"I wish I'd heard something from Tibbo," said Barney as they traveled along. "I haven't even had that prickly feeling since that first night we camped out."

"That's not all bad," Dick consoled him. "Maybe he's gone back to Ornam without you."

"Man! If only! But I don't think he'll go without saying good-bye. You know, even if he does always want things his way, I'll miss him."

"Ha!" said Dick. "Tibbo and his magic tricks. I don't trust him."

"Mom and Dad don't either." He was gradually becoming accustomed to thinking of the Crandalls as his parents. "They're invited to go to the MacDougalls' tonight after dinner. They have Kara coming to baby-sit with Scott so I can go with them. Isn't that wild? They act as if they're afraid Tibbo will snatch me the minute their backs are turned."

"Must be they believe in him now."

"I dunno. Maybe they just think I shouldn't be alone until I get over my weird ideas."

When Barney came into the house after ball practice, Mrs. Crandall was just turning away from the phone.

"That was Mrs. MacDougall," she said. "We'll be staying home tonight. Kara is coming down with a cold and they think she should go to bed early. Anyway, we wouldn't want Scott to catch the cold."

"Mom, I'll stay with Scott." Barney knew that the MacDougalls had also invited a new couple that had just moved up the road. They wanted them to meet the Crandalls. The party would be ruined, just because of him. Besides, in spite of the good refreshments he knew he'd share, he hadn't been looking forward to the evening with six grownups.

"I don't want to leave you," protested Mrs. Crandall.

Barney had an inspiration. "What if Dick came over?" He knew no one could save him from the Garks, but the Crandalls would feel better if he weren't alone, except for Scott.

"Well—that would be fine." Mrs. Crandall looked happier. "Tell him we won't be late, and we'll pick him up and drive him home."

It was a warm evening. After Scott was in bed and asleep, Dick and Barney sat on the back porch with the kitchen door open in case the little boy woke up.

The big porch was screened and equipped with comfortable chairs and a table.

After the afternoon of ball practice, Barney and Dick did not feel like playing the game of checkers that was ready on the table.

They sat and talked in a long cushioned swing that hung on chains fastened to the ceiling. Finn was curled up between them. Every now and then one of the boys put a foot to the floor to keep the swing moving.

Dick was telling about a vacation in Mexico with his parents. "You ought to see the pyramids down there," he was saying.

Barney was listening, full of interest, when another voice cut into Dick's conversation. The result was a jumble of words. Then the second voice became stronger.

"Barney! Come outside!" At the same moment Barney felt the all-too-familiar tingling of his skin.

Finn growled deep in his throat, and Barney sat up straight with his eyes wide and frightened.

"What is it?" asked Dick. "Tibbo?"

An icy fear clamped around Barney's heart. "He wants me to come outside." His voice was only a whisper.

Dick's eyes were full of blue fire. "Don't go!" he begged.

"Barney!" The voice came again. "I'm coming down in the mini ship. Now!"

Barney jumped to the floor and stood with clenched hands. "I'll be glad to see you. But I told you I'm not going to Ornam."

Tibbo went on talking as if he had not heard. "Don't bother to pack a bag. You won't even need a toothbrush."

"I'm not going!" Barney shouted.

Finn stood close beside Barney. Again he growled, and the hair on his back stood up like bristles.

"Look for a falling star!" called Tibbo. "That'll be me!"

"Dick! He won't listen!" cried Barney. "He's going to make me go to Ornam with him!"

But Dick had disappeared. Was that more of Tibbo's magic? Then in the silence Barney heard the sound of a phone being dialed. Dick was calling the Crandalls. That was good of him but they couldn't reach here in time. They had walked to MacDougalls', and it would take them at least ten or fifteen minutes to get home. By then he'd be gone.

Dick ran onto the porch. "They're coming! Mr. Mac-Dougall's driving them."

"They'd better hurry. Tibbo's on his way." Barney pointed to the sky. "He said to watch for a falling star."

The words had just left his mouth when a brilliant streak of light fell to earth like a golden rope. Seconds later a silver ball floated down, down, until it rested in the meadow behind the house. From the ring that was around the ball a sheet of silver dropped to the ground so the ball sat level and firm.

Dick drew in a long breath and let it out in an explosive, "Wow! I don't believe it!"

"Barney! Where are you?" Tibbo sounded cross. "The Garks are ready to leave!"

"You'll have to go without me." Barney spoke through lips that felt frozen.

Thoughts kept flying through his mind. If only the Crandalls were home. He wanted to see them once more. And Scott. How could he leave without giving him one last hug? Then he thought of Kara. He'd never date her now.

Dick had a firm grasp on his arm, and Finn McCool pressed close against him as if he, too, would hold him if he could.

Tibbo said, "It's natural for you to be uneasy. You've never been in a space ship." His voice was full of confidence. "You'll like it as soon as we're on our way. I know you will."

Barney did not answer, but he spoke softly to Dick. "He won't give up."

Dick whispered, "Run in the house and close the door. I'll stay out here and try to make him go away."

"Right," said Barney. Even though he knew he couldn't win against Tibbo's power, he was not going to leave without a fight.

With his eyes on the silver ship, he backed toward the open door to the kitchen.

20   FAREWELL

Dick raced across the porch and down the steps, letting the screen door slam behind him. He began to walk slowly across the grass toward the space ship.

Barney continued to back in the direction of the kitchen. At the same time he talked to Tibbo. "I wouldn't be good company for you on the trip," he said. "All the time I'd be thinking about the Earth and wishing I could be here. Go to Ornam without me, Tibbo. Please!"

Now he was in the kitchen doorway. He stretched out his left hand and locked his fingers behind the door frame. With his right hand he groped for the door, planning to slam it shut. But before he could reach it, a powerful force took control of his body.

Although he clung desperately to the edge of the doorway, his fingers slipped helplessly from the wood. Something was pulling him as easily as if he were a baby. When he came to the screen door some power turned the knob. Then the weight of his body pushed the door open and he bounced stiff legged down the steps.

Dick, who was ahead of him, spun around.

"I can't stop!" cried Barney. "Help me!"

Dick ran toward him, but when he was almost within reach he jolted to a stop and fell back as if he had hit a solid wall. He came forward again, and again he halted.

"I can't get to you!" he shouted. He hit the air with his fist but his hand leaped back. He clutched it as if it hurt.

Finn McCool, unable to open the screen door, was still on the porch, barking furiously.

Barney continued to move, slowly and steadily, toward the space ship. He couldn't think or speak, for he was using all of his energy to hold back. His heels dug twin paths through the grass, but nevertheless he was drawn nearer to the silver ship.

Behind him he heard the bang of the screen door. Then Scott called, "Barney! Wait!"

His brother's high, little-boy voice brought Barney out of his daze. "Tibbo! Let me go to Scott!" he pleaded. "I have to say good-bye to my brother."

At first he thought Tibbo was ignoring him. Then the pull on his body released so fast he fell backward to the ground.

"Hurry!" snapped Tibbo. "We're late now."

Barney flipped over and got onto one knee, but before he could stand up, he felt a warm tongue on his ear.

Finn had dashed outside when Scott opened the door. After giving the dog a quick hug, Barney scrambled to his feet and raced back to his brother. There he crouched down and wrapped his arms around the little fellow. He felt as if he could never let go.

Scott's face was wet. "Don't go away in that big ball!" he sobbed. "I heard you say you had to go."

Barney held him close. What could he do to comfort him? The touch of Finn McCool's paws on his shoulder gave him an idea.

"How'd you like to have a dog of your own?" he asked. "I'm going to give Finn to you."

"No! No!" Barney's offer seemed to make matters worse. "I want you!"

Again Barney felt the return of the terrible power that had pulled him out of the house. Now it drew him away from his brother, toward the space ship. All he could do was look back and wave and try to smile.

He was halfway to the silver ball when headlights swept into the driveway and the Crandalls jumped out of the car. They ran across the back lawn with Mrs. Crandall in the lead. Barney saw her fall and then get to her feet and keep on running. She was crying and screaming, "You can't take my son!"

At first Barney thought she was afraid Scott was going, too. But she sped past the little boy and stumbled on across the rough meadow.

The truth came to Barney like a fanfare of trumpets. *She's coming to me!*

Mr. Crandall caught up with her, and hand in hand they struggled forward. They acted as if something was restraining them.

A whirring sound from the space ship made Barney look toward it. A door was open and inside he could see a figure standing three or four feet back from the entrance. That must be Tibbo, he thought, but in the dim light he could not see the space boy clearly. He was only a not-very-tall shadow.

In another ten feet Barney would be at the open door. With a great effort he looked back over his shoulder.

"Mother! Dad!" he called. "Don't let me go!"

Suddenly they seemed to move more easily. In a moment their arms closed around him and he felt their wet faces against his.

So Tibbo was letting him say good-bye to them, too. Barney clung to them with a feeling of desperation.

"I'll never forget you," he promised. "I'll try to come back."

A wind blew against Barney's shoulders, reminding him that Tibbo was impatient to leave. This was the end. He knew there was nothing anyone could do to save him. He wrapped his arms more tightly around the Crandalls and waited for the strange force that would draw him into the ship.

The wind became stronger, blowing Barney's shirt against his back and making his hair stream forward.

"Look!" cried Mr. Crandall.

Barney turned. To his amazement he saw the silver skirt on which the ship had rested disappearing into the ring.

The shadowy figure of Tibbo was out of sight, for the door was closed.

As the ship began to rise, Barney stared at it with a sense of confusion. Was it actually going off into space without him?

Again Tibbo spoke to Barney. As usual no one else seemed to hear him. "I wish you were coming with me. But now I understand why you don't want to go. You've changed. You've become part of a family, and besides, there's Dick. You've found a true friend. I can't take you away."

The mist in Barney's eyes blurred the rapidly rising silver ball. Even though Tibbo had been only a voice, a mass of prickles, and finally a shadow, he, too, was a friend. Barney knew he would miss him.

"Will you come again?" he asked.

"I don't know, but I'll keep in touch. When you feel the prickles and hear me talk, will you answer?"

"Yes! Yes!"

The space ship became a tiny silver dot in the dark sky. Finally, it vanished.

The people who had watched the departure of the ship stood as if in a trance. Then, like a still picture turning into a movie, they began to walk about and to murmur to each other.

A moment later they again were motionless, listening, with heads lifted toward the sky, as Tibbo's voice floated clearly over the dark meadow: "Farewell, Earth Brother!"

ABOUT THE AUTHOR

Margaret Goff Clark lives just outside the city of Niagara Falls, near the Tuscarora Indian Reservation. At her adoption by the Senecas in July, 1962, she was given the Indian name of Deh-yi-sto-esh, meaning She Who Writes and Publishes.

Mrs. Clark says of herself, "I have been possessed by writing since I was a child." Her many poems, short stories, and one-act plays have appeared in newspapers, magazines, readers, and anthologies. She has written many books for young people. Ranging from mystery to historical fiction and biography, they reflect her enthusiasm for outdoor life, history, and travel.

After she was graduated from the State University College at Buffalo, she taught in the elementary grades and junior high school for six years.

The author is married to Charles R. Clark, a former classmate in college. They are the parents of two children, Robert, a radiologist in Walnut Creek, California, and Marcia, a nurse in Los Angeles. When they are not trailering around the United States, the Clarks vacation at their cottage in Ontario, Canada.